ADVANCE PRAISE FOR

More of This World or Maybe Another

by Barb Johnson

"These are stunning stories. Barb [illegible] of writer whose work I dream of finding and [illegible]es, precise and gorgeous language. Yes, a wonderful sense of humor, and another of pathos made over into something much more effective—a vision of all these people just doing the best they can and along the way becoming the best kind of stories—the kind that reveal, enlarge, and make living seem worth the trouble."

—Dorothy Allison, author of *Bastard Out of Carolina*

"Barb Johnson's beautiful and touching stories stirred up emotions in me that few books ever have. . . . I hate to admit it, [but] I actually cried over a pig in one of the stories, and I used to work in a meatpacking plant!"

—Donald Ray Pollock, author of *Knockemstiff*

"What a wickedly fine debut *More of This World or Maybe Another* is. Barb Johnson, a great new talent, brings both the familiar and the extraordinary to life on every page. Once you're introduced to characters like Delia or Luis, they will haunt you for a very long time. With her first collection, Johnson proves herself a master of the short story."

—Joseph Boyden, author of *Three Day Road* and *Through Black Spruce*

"Barb Johnson's stories are stark yet lit with an imaginative power that will not allow us to look away from the truths she depicts. Many of the titles are savagely ironic: "More of This World or Maybe Another," "Killer Heart," and "St. Luis of Palmyra." Johnson's achievement in this collection is richly compelling."

—Gerald Duff, author of *Coasters* and *Fire Ants*

More of This World or Maybe Another

More of This World or Maybe Another

Barb Johnson

HARPER PERENNIAL

NEW YORK • LONDON • TORONTO • SYDNEY • NEW DELHI • AUCKLAND

For Virginia Sonnier

And for Mid-City—
heart of New Orleans,
heart of my heart

P.S.™ is a trademark of HarperCollins Publishers.

FIRST EDITION

Library of Congress Cataloging-in-Publication Data is available upon request.

ISBN 978-0-06-173227-0

20 OV/LSC 10 9 8 7 6 5 4 3

Contents

More of This World or Maybe Another

Delia has to walk past A. J. Higginbotham and his crowd to get to the gym, which is where the dance is. The boys are installed on the railing under the long breezeway like they're at a livestock auction, cans of Skoal wearing their way through back pockets. Delia raises her right hand and shoots the bird at the lineup for the entire fifty-foot walk.

Pup-py Chow for a ful-l-l-l year—till she's full grown! A.J. sings as the group of girls behind Delia passes him. Higginbothams. Fuckers don't know enough to keep off each other. All eight inbred Higginbotham brothers and sisters are in high school at the same time. A.J. is in Delia's remedial math class, his second go-round. They'll probably pass him this time. If they don't, there'll be a Higginbotham logjam next year, and their teacher said she won't put up with more than two Higginbothams at a time. Frick and Frack. One in the front and one in the back.

Delia pushes through the crowd bunched up at the door, scopes the gym for her friend, Calvin, and his twin sister, Charlene. Charlene—everyone calls her Chuck—drove Calvin to the dance an hour early so he could help set up the sound system. Chuck drives an old Valiant, paid for with her own money, Calvin said. He didn't say how she got the money, but Delia knows it has something to do with the weed that can be bought at the caretaker's shed behind the old Blue Moon Drive-In.

There's no sign of Calvin, but Delia sees Chuck right away, glowing, high above the crowd in the bleachers. She's sitting with a group of girls who are a blur of heavy eyeliner and large hoop earrings, girls who laugh really loud at just anything. Chuck, though, she's like a bright red engine light in a dark car for how she can get your full attention without making a sound. Everyone knows she keeps a switchblade in one of her boots. Delia licks her lips, which have gone suddenly dry, and weaves her way toward the bleachers.

She's not sure what the arrangement for tonight is, but she hopes that she and Calvin are not supposed to be on some kind of date. There are plenty of girls who would love to date Calvin Lafleur. He got left back when they were in junior high, so he's a year older than the other boys in the junior class. The baby fat in his face is gone, but there's still plenty of it in his head. He's always bragging about how often he has to shave, like it's some kind of accomplishment. The other girls fall for it, but Delia could give a damn. She wants other things. Things she doesn't even know the name of. And anyway, she'd hate to ruin her and Calvin's friendship with a bunch of dating rigamarole. Since her best friend, Renée, has gone all boy-crazy, Calvin is about the only one who'll go with Delia to the pasture out on the highway and sneak rides on the Higginbothams' horses. Sometimes Calvin's friends come. And, lately, Chuck.

"Seen the meat?" Delia calls up from the bottom riser when

Chuck finally looks away from the group of girls. Chuck's eyes are black-black, and looking into them gives Delia a feeling like driving without headlights at night, like speeding down one of the mile roads that separate the rice fields at the edge of town where she lives.

Chuck flicks a sheet of hair, dark and liquid, over her shoulder. "The meat's in the dressing room smoking a doobie," she says. "Why? You looking to dance?"

"Might be," Delia says and stares through the gaps in the bleachers.

Chuck scoots away from the other girls. "Wouldn't be a date without some dancing," she says. "Or maybe you're after a kiss?"

Delia looks in the direction of the locker room. Looks at Chuck. "Maybe," she says.

Chuck waves Delia up. Her hands are muscular and look like they're built to do something very specific. The top half of her right index finger is missing, and this makes Delia think of the switchblade in Chuck's boot. She wonders if it came before the stumpy finger or after. She studies the fleshy nub the way she's caught people studying the hot-grease scar on her own forehead. Behind Delia's bangs, there's a medallion of skin from her upper thigh that was laid over a grease burn she got when she was five. It's the same size and color as a Ritz cracker now. Her head has grown, but the skin graft has only stretched. It looks like a shiny, wrinkled eyelid up there.

The band starts an out-of-tune version of "Crimson and Clover," and a strobe light flashes above the stage. Very psychedelic. Chuck's friends scatter like buckshot, snagging boys to dance with. *My, my such a sweet thing . . .* Delia holds her breath. *I want to do ev-er-y-thing . . .* She imagines herself singing this to someone.

Could she? She wonders if other girls wonder these things. When the band gets to the song's stuttering refrain, Delia sings along, batting an index finger against her throat: *O-O-O-Over and O-O-O-Over . . .* Chuck looks at Delia and laughs, a sound that runs down Delia's spine like a message in code. Then Chuck works her stumpy finger against her own throat, and Delia sees that half an index finger is plenty to do what needs doing in life.

After the song is over, Calvin staggers out of the boys' dressing room, and he and his friends shuffle in the general direction of Delia and Chuck. "Cyclops," he says to Delia on his way up to the top of the bleachers.

"Meat," Delia returns, pushing her bangs up and flashing the third eye of scar at him.

Calvin and his crowd settle in on the top row of the bleachers, several levels above Delia and Chuck. Delia's mother made her wear a dress to the dance, and in between songs, Delia overhears Calvin and his friends discussing the ease of access created by this fact. She makes a noise like a pig, a sound so realistic that farm animals have been fooled by it. Calvin and his pals start up barking. There's a pretty big difference between how Calvin acts when it's just him and Delia, and how he gets when he's around his friends. A couple of weeks ago, when they were alone, Calvin told Delia that if he ever got drafted, he wasn't going. "It's just wrong, you know? The military? It's messed up. I'm gonna dodge." Delia's brother has recently returned from the war, so nobody ever talks about skipping out on the military around her. "I'll drive you to Canada myself," she told Calvin, and that's when he tried to kiss her, spoiling a perfectly good moment.

Delia thinks about the future when she'll likely have to marry one of the idiots behind her, or somewhere in this room, at least.

She can never imagine how it will happen, but she knows that one day she'll wake up in a house full of Higginbothams or Lafleurs and not have one clue how she got there. Or why she hates it, which she knows she will.

In between songs, Chuck reaches over and taps Delia's knee with her stumpy finger. "It's okay if you want to go up there and talk with Calvin," she says, tipping her head back toward the boys.

"Hell no," Delia says. "Bunch of idiots." She can feel the place where Chuck touched her leg, as though she's been stamped with the heated coil of a car's cigarette lighter instead of the wrinkled tip of Chuck's stubby finger.

A few songs later, Calvin comes down from the top of the bleachers and squeezes in between Chuck and Delia. "You want to dance?" he yells to Delia over the music.

"Nah," Delia hollers back, not taking her eyes off the dance floor, "I'm stag." When Chuck was trying to convince Delia to come to the dance a while back, she said, "I'm going stag." Delia has no idea what *stag* means. It seems like maybe it's a category. Like there are girls who want to be on a date. And girls who don't. Saying "stag" lets people know which kind of girl you are. "Besides," Delia tells Calvin now, giving him a pig snort, "I don't dance with livestock."

"Suit yourself," Calvin says, turning and climbing back up the bleachers to his pals. Delia knows it doesn't matter to him one way or the other whether they dance together. He's probably only asked her on a dare. Recently, it seems as though Delia's whole class has turned into a bunch of cattle for how they only do what everyone else is doing or daring them to do.

After Calvin leaves, Chuck taps Delia's knee again and points to the dance floor. Delia's soon-to-be-ex–best friend, Renée, is dancing with a boy she began seeing a few weeks ago, which is exactly how long it's been since Delia's seen Renée anywhere but at the bus stop or on the bus.

"I let him go all the way," Renée wrote in the back of her notebook one morning last week. She held the page between them on the bus seat so Delia could read it. When Delia didn't say anything back, Renée leaned in closer. "I finally lost my virginity," she whispered, cupping one hand around Delia's ear. "Can you believe it?" Why wouldn't Delia believe it? It's cause and effect. If you have sex, you lose your virginity. "It's really beautiful," Renée went on in her new prissy-wise voice. "You'll see." All the way to school, Delia thought about that phrase, about "letting" someone go all the way. It made sex sound like something Renée had to put up with instead of enjoy. Like how Delia dressed in three heavy coats one Christmas and "let" Pooky Langlois shoot at her with his new BB gun. Pooky gave her five dollars, so it was worth it. She wonders what Renée got.

Right this minute, Renée's draped over the boyfriend out on the dance floor, swaying off-beat to the music. The boyfriend, Renée has explained, is her best friend. She can tell him anything. Delia imagines this is probably the end of the line for her and Renée, and she turns her head away from the dancers.

When Chuck goes off to the bathroom, Delia goes to get some punch for both of them. While she's ladling the fruit and liquid into the cups, A. J. Higginbotham asks her to dance.

"I'm stag," Delia tells him.

"The hell you are," A.J. says and starts barking, which starts the other boys barking. Barking is the new thing this year. It's like there was a meeting this past summer, and the boys all agreed that the girls would enjoy a full year of dog talk.

When Delia gets back to the bleachers, she hands over one of the cups of punch to Chuck, who has moved closer to the dance floor. Chuck frowns at the delicate paper cup and downs the whole drink in a few gulps. Delia settles in next to her and turns her attention to where A.J. and another boy are poking their scrawny chests out at each other. A crowd gathers around them in hopes of seeing a fight. *Idiots.* When Delia looks at Chuck again, she's carved her initials into the side of the empty punch cup, which means she's pulled the switchblade from her boot and done the carving without Delia ever seeing it. Delia wonders what else she's missed.

After a while, Chuck leans over and says, "You want to go have a smoke in the car?" Her voice is close, and her breath is moist against Delia's ear. Delia pretends she doesn't understand, waits to see if Chuck is going to invite others along because Delia's not about to be trapped in a car with the hoop-earring-and-eyeliner catpack.

Delia goes back to watching Renée on the dance floor. Chuck gives her a nudge and points again in the direction of the parking lot with a question on her face. Another girl might favor her good hand, might keep that stump out of sight. Does Chuck use that finger to dial the phone, Delia wonders, staring at the wriggling stub, or has she learned to get the phone dialed some other way?

When they get to the gravel lot behind the gym, Chuck's rusty Valiant is backed up to the edge where matches flash and die like fireflies, and all the loud talk defeats the purpose of hiding out behind the building.

The car's dashboard is swollen and split, its stuffing exposed. Below the dash, on the ledge in front of the speedometer, is about half a tightly rolled fatty. Right out in the open.

"Roll up your window, would you?" Chuck asks. "We don't need to listen to all that jackassness going on out there."

Delia tries to think of a question she can ask to get the conversation going. She picks at a brittle flap of dashboard skin just over the radio. "Radio work?" she asks. Music is a way to be with someone but not.

Chuck looks at the radio, clicks the knob on and off, on and off. When the clicking stops, there's just quiet again.

Delia sneaks a look across the front seat to see whether the silence is bothering Chuck or whether she likes it. Chuck seems fine, and Delia turns to watch people from the dance stumbling out the back door of the gym. Rich kids in their designer clothes—Mr. and Miss Everything. A few hippies. Ten or so goat ropers in their dress cowboy hats, pearl-snap shirts, tight jeans and boots. The stream of ropers pools around the car parked next to Chuck and Delia. Boys in one group. Girls in another. Even goat-roper girls aren't interested in watching their dates spit tobacco juice. Instead, they start up a high-pitched debate about barrel racing.

Slowly, the windshield of Chuck's car fogs up, and Delia slouches in her seat, low, then lower, so she can watch through a small clear patch.

"I guess we better put the windows down," Chuck says when there's no clear space left. "People are going to think we're in here making out."

Delia's face heats up, and she turns it toward her open window in case Chuck can tell. Over against the gym, a couple of hippies have begun making out. How do you know when to close your eyes for a kiss, Delia wonders. What if both people close their eyes, but no one leans in? What if you lean in, and the other person turns away?

While she's watching the hippies, Delia hears the *flink* of Chuck opening her lighter and the scritching of the spark wheel against the flint. She turns back expecting to see Chuck lighting the joint, but just as a flame appears, Chuck flips the cap shut. She does it again and then again so that the sound of it is like a conversation. Like Chuck's saying something and Delia's listening.

A ship's horn sounds out on the river a couple of miles away. Two blasts: something big passing something small. The big ship, a freighter probably, will dock downriver from Delia's house, and all night big blue cranes will load rice or soybeans or oil into its hold. Food and petroleum are forever on the way to parts of the world Delia is afraid she will never see.

"You 'bout done?" Chuck asks. Out of the blue, it seems to Delia, and way too soon. Done with the dance, Delia supposes Chuck means. Or maybe done sitting in the car? Everything Chuck says could be this thing or that thing, or even a thing Delia has never heard of.

While Delia's still trying to figure out the question, Chuck lights the joint. She leans over to shotgun it for Delia, and Delia pulls back. She rubs at her eye like the smoke got in it until Chuck backs off the shotgun pose and hands over the joint. Delia inhales and holds the smoke until her lungs burn so she can be sure the high will take hold. Eventually, whatever was snagged, turned sideways in her, settles to the bottom like an anchor. She can hear A.J. and the boys around the corner of the gym. *Puppy Chow for a ful-l-l year* . . . they're singing to some girl. To any girl. It's like A.J. doesn't know he's a buck-toothed, inbred bastard. He acts like the whole world is his to comment on.

They pass the joint back and forth without talking, Delia, then Chuck. Each time they let smoke out of their lungs, it hangs between them for a second like something solid that's been said, that needs thinking about before it goes back to being just air.

This might be it, Delia thinks when they finish the joint. This might be all. "You want to go to Emerald City?" she blurts out, turning toward the open window quick like she's caught sight of something interesting. The pot has made time all screwy, and Delia makes herself count to ten before she says anything else. "I know where there's an empty tank," she says. Empty tanks are the best. No mucky oil. No killer stink of petroleum.

Chuck runs her fingers through her hair. "Emerald City," she says, then reaches over the seat and pulls a set of amber-colored Clackers up by a single string. She hands them to Delia. An answer.

Emerald City is what they call the tank farms across the river where miles of oil-storage tanks, like thirty-foot-tall cans of tuna, are laid out in a petrochemical subdivision. Anyone can climb the stairs up the side of one, open the door, and go on in. It's best to bring along flashlights and Clackers and mushrooms pinched from beneath cow pies. An old sheet if you have it. Turn the flashlight off and smack the Clackers together—*click-clack, click-clack*—until the high, sharp echo shakes you loose from yourself and lifts you up out of this world and into another.

Holding the Clackers up, Delia asks, "Who'd you get these from?" They're chipped, a telltale sign that they've been smacked together too hard and too long. In whose hands, Delia wonders. When?

"Oh, I've had those quite a while," Chuck says.

There's the sound of a key sliding in the ignition. Delia can hear each tooth shoving the pins of the lock aside. She watches Chuck's hand turn the starter, and the Valiant's busted muffler roars to the crowd behind the gym. The goat ropers jump a mile high and yell something at the car. Words she can't hear. Barnyard words probably.

The sharp, bright curves of Chuck's movie star profile cut into the dark outside the window. She gets dimples at the corners of her mouth when she smiles, which is not all that often. Though she's smiling at Delia now. She lets up on the gas, and the muffler quiets to a low rumble. "You ready?" she asks.

Emerald City. Anything could be out there. Things Delia doesn't want. Or the things she does want but isn't sure she'll recognize if she sees them. "What about the meat?" she says, hedging.

"What about him?" Chuck yells over the monster truck sound of the broken muffler as they peel out onto the highway.

About a month ago, they'd all been riding horses in the Higginbothams' pasture. Calvin and his friends and Chuck and Delia and Renée. There's a sweet mare they call Pollyanna, and a little monkey-see-monkey-do broke out when Calvin vaulted neatly onto the animal's bare back. And then Chuck and then everyone else except Delia and Renée.

"Oh, I could never do that," Renée said in the pouty, dumb-girl voice she'd recently started using. Delia hated how Renée flirted with boys by going all wiggly and dense.

The horses didn't belong to them, so they'd given them whatever names seemed to fit. One, Jack the Ripper, a stallion who none of them had ever been able to ride, sneered at the group from the edge of the activity. While everyone else was busy with Polyanna, Delia crept around the edge of the pasture until she was standing behind Jack. Closing her mind to the many reasons not to, she took off running straight at his hindquarters. Miraculously, she landed on his back, a brief victory before he tore out into the middle of the pasture and tried to scrape her off with a low tree branch. When that didn't work, he sprinted straight at the barbed-wire fence and stopped short of it, pitching Delia over into the blackberry bushes on the other side.

Renée got to her first, but Chuck was right behind.

"You're just showing off for Calvin," Renée said, hand turned backward on her hip. Hip jutting out. A rich-girl pose she copied from the Miss Everythings at school. "Why can't you flirt like a normal girl?"

Something about that made Chuck smile. And there were the dimples.

As soon as Renée was sure that Delia wasn't actually hurt, she turned toward the barbed-wire fence and made a big production of getting not one, but two, of the boys to help her back over into the pasture.

Chuck sat down next to Delia, who really was hurt but wasn't about to give Renée the satisfaction of seeing it. They picked blackberries right where they sat and ate them, the *ka-thunk* of nearby oil wells giving a rhythm to their conversation.

"If you asked Calvin to the Sadie Hawkins dance," Chuck said, popping a berry into her mouth and licking her purpled fingers, "we could all ride together."

The other girls in Delia's class were excited because a Sadie Hawkins dance, their teacher explained, meant that the girls got to do the inviting instead of the boys. Like everything else about this school year, Delia couldn't understand what the big deal was. She wasn't going.

"I'm going stag," Chuck added.

Delia picked a few blackberries and ate them. "I'll go stag, too," she said, deciding she wanted more of the feeling she had sitting there with Chuck among the stickers and the berries. "But I'm going to take my daddy's truck," she added, "in case it's boring." In case the feeling she was having couldn't be had anywhere but there among the blackberries, where everything boring had gone back to the other side of the barbed-wire fence.

When Chuck steers the Valiant out onto the dark highway, Delia stares into the nothingness. She thinks of cities where there must be stoplights at least. Buildings lit up at night with people in them making the city go. She dreams of roads that aren't bordered by ditches, by the segmented crescents of dead armadillos. Places where the night doesn't press down on you the way it's pressing down on her now, like it's water she might drown in if she doesn't pay attention. Up ahead, a blue light marks the location of a firebox. It's hitched to the pole where the highway turns onto the parish road. They fishtail around the corner, swimming through the faint blue glow, and drive all the way to the bridge with the lights off.

Except for the flashing red beacon at the top, the steep, two-lane bridge is unlit, its downside all but invisible, a matter of faith. As a child, Delia used to hide in the car's foot well when her family drove to visit her cousins who live on the other side of the river. "There're two sides to a bridge, Delia," her mother used to tell her when Delia scrambled for the foot well. "That's what a bridge is."

Maybe so, Delia thought, but things can change with no warning and still look exactly the same. Delia's oldest brother went off to fight in the war. A crazy man who screams and cries when you drop a pot in the kitchen came back in his place. He looks like Delia's brother, but he's not. It looks like a bridge, but maybe it isn't.

From the top of the bridge, Delia can see the tanks of Emerald City lined up like a marching band behind the drum major of the natural gas refinery whose signal baton is a forty-foot torch that burns off the flare emissions. The flame goes up and then shrinks, all the while bending with the wind. Delia slouches in her seat and closes one eye. It looks like the flame is coming out of the stump of Chuck's index finger, which is resting against the steering wheel. When Delia switches eyes, the flame jumps out of the car's window. If it ever goes out, Delia's been told, the whole town will be blown sky high. It could go out. It could go out right this minute with her and Chuck in the car at the top of the bridge. It could go out now. Or now. There's no way to know ahead of time.

When they get to the tank farm, they slip through a loose corner of the chain-link fence that surrounds it. Everyone knows about the loose spot except the refinery people. The tank farm is the closest Delia's ever been to a city with big buildings. Walking in the shadows of the giant tanks makes Delia's heart squeeze too much blood up to her head, so that it feels like her brain is going to come blasting out of her ears.

She and Chuck are both stoned, and Chuck keeps tripping and grabbing Delia's shoulder as they make their way down the rough oyster-shell lane. Delia fakes a near fall to see what it feels like to touch Chuck back. When she does, her hand lands on Chuck's wrist, which feels solid but much smaller than Delia imagined.

It's windy there among the tanks and quiet, except for the sound of the refineries, a clanking, hissing sound, a sound like a big brain working. In the sky, a yellow cloud of sulfur is backlit and hangs in the air like a ghost above the bridge, whose massive underside is straight out of a nightmare. Delia cannot begin to guess what it is that's keeping that bridge from collapsing under its own weight.

"How can you tell which tank's empty?" Chuck asks. She's stopped in the middle of the shell lane, and Delia stops beside her.

Like all of Chuck's questions, this one could mean a lot of things. Maybe she's giving Delia the chance to show off. Or she might be trying to catch Delia in a lie.

Delia has lied. She has no idea how to tell which tank is empty. She thought that saying she did would make her seem more experienced than she is, would make the plan sound more exciting to Chuck. Delia jerks her head in the direction of the tank to their left. "Watch this," she says. Plucking the Clackers from around Chuck's neck, she uses them to give the tank a few knocks. "Hear that? That's how they sound when they're full." Delia's not ready to stop yet. It's like she and Chuck are in some magic world that might actually have a perfect tank in it. One they won't find if they stop too soon. "The empty one's farther down the road."

After passing twenty or so of the giant round tanks, Delia stops in front of one whose seams are smooth, new enough not to have grown any rust. Fresh shells around the base. Maybe full, maybe empty. It's not like she can really tell the difference. She wants to confess the stupid lie. But a lie is just words, she guesses, and so is a confession. "This is it," Delia says, and just saying it makes it so.

Chuck gives the tank a drum roll with the Clackers, pulls her hair over one shoulder and braids it. "Hold this a minute," she says, and hands Delia the braid while she secures the end with a twist tie, the kind that comes on a bread wrapper. Something about the feel of the silky plait embarrasses Delia, and she looks back down the road. Shifts nervously from side to side.

"What?" Chuck asks about the shifting.

Delia flips the fastened braid over Chuck's shoulder. "What what?" Delia asks and it sounds funny, the way everything does when she's stoned. "What what," she says again, and it's even funnier.

Chuck shrugs and starts up the metal stairs that curve around the huge tank. Delia falls in behind her. Halfway up, there's the crunch of tires on oyster shells. Theron Higginbotham—A.J.'s uncle—works security for the refinery. "There's just no getting away from those peckers," Delia says.

Chuck keeps climbing. "Which peckers?"

Delia presses her back against the tank, grabs the hem of Chuck's skirt to stop her. "Hold up." The sight of Chuck's bare thighs gives Delia a feeling like lying, a blast of adrenaline that dissolves in a pool of guilt.

Theron's headlights bounce along the shell road. "Lights on," Chuck says, "but nobody's home."

Delia looks down, and already that world seems small and strange. The world of the tank is the real world now. She's queasy with excitement.

"We're up here, igmo!" Chuck hollers at the back of Theron's truck as it disappears around a corner. "Come on up and let's make out!"

"If that idiot comes back," Delia warns, "I'm leaving your ass right here and taking your car."

"They made Theron register at the post office, Delia. That old boy's not allowed anywhere near minors."

"Oh, yeah," Delia says, like she's remembering this detail, though she has no idea what Chuck is talking about. She lets go of Chuck's hem, which she may have been holding on to longer than necessary.

When they reach the top of the stairs, three stories up, they stand on a small platform, their shoulders nearly touching. Delia squints at the view. Everything's out of proportion, and it makes her feel big and small at the same time. Chuck starts the Clackers going, *click-clack, click-clack, click-clack*, a noise like a train coming or an idea.

A red light flashes on the top of each storage tank to keep the crop dusters from running into them, long strings of red marking some higher road. Delia imagines stepping out onto it, following it to see where it goes.

Across the river a scatter of lights. The high school's over there, and beyond that, Delia's house, which, if she could see it, would be in a dark field, surrounded by other dark fields, lit only by the pale fruit of egrets sleeping in the trees along the bayou. Everything is so small and far away. If she went into her house right now, she imagines it would be like when she tried to put a regular-sized doll in the dollhouse her father made for her. If she went in her house right now, she couldn't tuck her own long legs under the dinner table without flipping the thing over, the tiny plates spilling the food that will never be enough again. She imagines the clothes in her closet and sees doll clothes, her bed, a shoebox that would collapse beneath her.

In the other direction, night is rolled out as far as Delia can see. There's a swamp out there, she knows, and the Gulf of Mexico. Beyond that, there could be anything. More of this world or maybe another.

When the Clackers go quiet, Delia turns and faces Chuck. She reaches over and wraps her fingers around the brass handle of the tank's door, composes an explanation in case the tank isn't empty. In case that matters to Chuck. But then she thinks about the darkness and the echo behind the door, a door to a place she's already been, and lets go of the handle. Like a small bird flying into the wind, Delia's hand migrates toward Chuck, skittering to a stop on the slope of Chuck's waist, shaky from the trip.

Seconds unwind in slow motion while Delia's heart does a bangity-bang against her ribs, Clackers going too fast, too hard.

Chuck lifts her right hand with its half finger and moves it toward her own waist, toward Delia's hand there. Chuck will hold it, or she will move it aside.

Delia will lean in for a kiss or turn away.

Now.

Or now.

Keeping Her Difficult Balance

Everything floats down to this place, the very end of Bayou St. John where Delia sits, her feet dangling just above the tepid water. An egret pecks at a bread wrapper that's washed ashore. Delia is comforted by the filth of the city. She loves the fact of this bayou, which is right smack in the middle of New Orleans, surrounded by streets and houses. Not at all like the one from her childhood in the boonies of East Jesus. She tilts her head against her boyfriend—her fiancé—Calvin's thick, bare triceps, which he flexes just a little any time he thinks someone will notice. Like now. The muscle rises where Delia's cheek is resting on it, tugging her face into a half smile. She pulls away.

"What you so grumpy about?" Calvin asks.

Delia looks across the water to a group of trailers huddled along the edge of the bayou. "I hate that word," she says. "Grumpy." She draws out the *g-r-r* part of it. It's true. She is grumpy. Who knows why.

Calvin works at Spanky's Automotive, right here on the bayou, and most Fridays, Delia walks down to meet him after work. Now he unbuttons the navy blue shirt of his uniform, which he has customized by cutting off the sleeves. He wipes his pits with it and sets it aside. "Better?" he asks.

When Delia doesn't say anything, he digs through his box of catalpa worms and baits his hook, casts his line. He knows something's up. It seems to Delia that every time they get to a place where she might say what it is, might even say, "That's it. We're done," Calvin lapses into Caveman. Mr. Twitching Muscles. Mr. Cloudy Perception.

"Something happen at the Laundromat?" Calvin asks. A safe question. Delia has started her own Laundromat right here in Mid-City. Every day something crazy happens.

"It's the bridal shower," she sighs. Her mother and aunts are throwing Delia a shower in Gremillion, where she and Calvin grew up. It's a month off, still, but once she accepts the presents, the wedding's a done deal. Delia's not sure it's a deal she wants to make. "I wish I didn't have to go."

"Because of the dizziness, you mean?" Calvin asks.

"Yeah, that's it," Delia says and closes her eyes against Mr. Cloudy Perception. "I don't want to go home because of the dizziness." A few weeks ago, while Delia was changing a fluorescent tube in the Laundromat, she fell off a ladder and hit her head. She's been having bouts of vertigo ever since. "Calvin?"

"You got to keep your eyes on the prize, baby," Calvin says, cutting Delia off. "You got to stay focused on the booty, the take, the haul."

Delia can tell that Calvin doesn't want to get into whatever it is that's bothering her. "Right," she says. "Because I'm all about the haul."

"That's my girl," Caveman says. He puts his heavy arm around Delia and pulls her to him.

Every time Delia complains about the shower, her mother says the same thing: You and Calvin deserve a good start. Delia and Calvin have been living together for almost two years. What could they possibly need? Matching towels and kitchen appliances Delia will never use? If people want to give them a prize for fucking, Delia would rather have a stack of cash to take on their honeymoon to San Francisco. They're going to spend a week with Calvin's twin sister, Charlene, who everyone calls Chuck. Back in high school, Chuck and Delia were pretty close.

Chuck and her roommate, Jin, a Chinese girl Chuck met at her job, actually live in Oakland. San Francisco is right there across the bridge, is what Chuck said. She sent a letter with pictures of her and Jin in front of places Delia can't wait to see. *Y'all come stay with us*, Chuck wrote in neat square letters. *We'll tear this place up!* Neither Calvin nor Delia has laid eyes on Chuck since they graduated high school two years ago. In the pictures, Chuck looks different than Delia remembers. Happier, she guesses. She signed her letter, *Love, Chuck and Jin.*

Delia watches Calvin cast his line again. He swings his legs out and lets his heels smack against the cement bulkhead and then sings along with their bounce. Bow, chicka-bow, chicka-bow-bowww. Thinking of Chuck and the trip to San Francisco puts Delia's mood on the upswing. She takes a deep breath and vows again to quit being so cranky with Calvin and to let his happy-man-fishing mood seep into her. She rests her cheek against his flexing triceps and follows the rising curve of his fishing pole from its base in his big hands, whose nails are never clean, to the very tip, which, from Delia's perspective, seems to be resting among the trailers on the opposite shore. Big Luce, the woman she rents the Laundromat from, lives over there. It's a single city block of bohemia on the water. Seven trailers curve along the bayou in a bright, white toothy smile with a single silver cap, a tiny Airstream, right in the front.

If Delia were a quarter inch tall, she could walk up the long slope of Calvin's fishing pole and down to the fine tip, a springboard that would bounce her right into the center of those trailers. Just like that, she could walk into some other life. In her mind, Delia descends from the fishing-pole bridge and steps into the middle of the trailers, where she takes a seat on one of the cypress stumps and waits for the artists to come out and join her. She imagines the artists telling her how they all found each other. Whether all the trailers arrived together or if maybe, one at a time, people realized they belonged there and got themselves a trailer and moved it into the circle.

Suddenly Calvin's arm tightens under Delia's cheek, and he pulls back on the pole, winding in line. "I got you now, hoss!" he says, his voice going suddenly high with excitement. Scratch Calvin, and you'll find a rosy-cheeked little boy just below the surface, one of the many things that Delia admires about him. Whenever she's around Calvin, all the wobble goes out of the world's orbit, and everything seems clear and easy. "It's only as complicated as you make it, baby," he often tells her.

Delia reaches behind her for the net and sets it next to Calvin. She'd rather disappear for this portion of the program—flailing-fish-meets-net—not just because of what is about to happen to some poor, unsuspecting fish, but because Calvin requires an audience. Someone has to see him fight the fish and win. It's a fish with a minuscule brain. Delia can't imagine why anyone would want a witness. And it's not that Calvin comes right out and says, Watch me. It's just a rule. Women have to watch men. It's exhausting.

While Calvin, who is six-two, wrestles a fifteen-inch catfish, a red canoe gets loose from its tie-up on the opposite shore. The artists aren't outside, and, for a while, Delia's the only one who knows about the boat's getaway plans. She tracks the progress of the little canoe, knows that nothing really needs to be done about it. The water will bring it right here to the end of the bayou and push it up on land. You don't have to tie down every single thing to keep track of it.

"Oh, man," Calvin says when he sees the canoe. "Some jackass didn't tie his boat up."

Delia points across to the tiny trailer park. "Came from over there," she says. "They'll know where to find it."

"Well, no, Delia. When the tide shifts, it's going to carry it clear to the lake." Delia doubts this, but Calvin likes to solve problems, and you can't solve a problem unless there is one.

He lowers the hooked catfish into the grass, puts one of his big boots across its body and works the barb loose from inside the fish's mouth. The catfish struggles against the pain of the hook, which Calvin swears it can't feel, and gasps for oxygen, which there's plenty of, though none the fish can use. "Why don't you paddle it back over for them?" Calvin asks.

Delia looks away from the gasping fish. "Why don't you?" The embarrassing fact is that Delia is afraid of boats, one of the many things she's never told Calvin, who assumes everyone is living a rational life. I'm afraid of boats, she imagines telling him. But you can swim, he'd argue. I'm not afraid of drowning, Delia would answer.

I'm afraid of falling. I'm afraid I'll tip the boat and fall in. But you can swim, he'd repeat. In Calvin's mind, the best way to correct wrong thinking is through the repetition of a fact. There's no explaining yourself to him.

Calvin tosses the catfish in a bucket of water with another fish, then hops into the red canoe and paddles off. He won't just bring the boat back; he'll have to find the owner and explain the error of his ways. Sure enough, after he ties the boat up, Delia hears the faint echo of his *Hello? Hello?*

A girl comes out of the little silver Airstream and, *flip-flap, flip-flap,* walks over to Calvin. She's tall and moves the way that rich girls who've had ballet lessons move, loose in the hips, feet pointing out. She puts her hands up to her face in an expression of what Delia would say is false embarrassment. It's the expression girls give to guys when they're trying to move things along. It's faster than arguing. Her body language is pitch-perfect, designed to save Calvin's feelings. You're trying to be helpful, the girl's body says, and I'm trying to look embarrassed by what you perceive as my neglect, which is what you want from me. Calvin's body says, I'm a superhero. It's my duty to rescue, ma'am, and to explain the world to you.

There's a frantic splashing in the bucket next to Delia, and she's sure one of the fish is about to jump out and swim away. The struggle doesn't last, though. The catfish go quiet in their murky prison. They've accepted their fate, Delia imagines. *Que sera, sera.*

Delia backs her little Toyota truck up onto the sidewalk in front of the Bubble, which is what she has finally decided to call her Laundromat. She's been too nervous about falling to get up on a ladder and hang the sign she made. At the service entrance, she doesn't even have the key in the lock before her buddy, Pudge, is behind her. He's Big Luce's nephew, and the Laundromat is home base, the place he's said he spent most of his time as a child, when Big Luce ran her own Laundromat out of this building.

"You need help with that?" Pudge asks, meaning the two used coin-op washers in the back of the truck.

Pudge enjoys breakfast cocktails, which often makes him a little dangerous as a helper. He looks bleary but not unsteady this morning. "I could use some help if you've got a few minutes," Delia says. She wishes Pudge would take money when he helps her, which is often, but he won't. She doesn't like to feel beholden, like she's been helped because she's a girl. "I'm happy to take a beer," Pudge always tells her. "Cuts out the middleman, if you know what I mean."

Delia goes inside. While she's digging through the storage area for the dolly, she hears yelling coming from the front of the Laundromat. On Palmyra Street, saying hello and fighting can sound just alike, and it's pretty time-consuming if you investigate every loud conversation.

"Put it back!" she hears a woman yell. "I'll call the cops. You better put it back."

Delia runs down the side of the building to the front, where she finds Pudge with his hands up. He's spindly, emaciated, except for a nearly round basketball of beer gut under his T-shirt. One of the washers is off the truck in the street next to him. A girl straddles a bike with a bag of groceries on the back, her finger aimed at Pudge like a gun. She's wearing those sandals—Delia doesn't know the name of them—the kind that cost a couple hundred bucks.

"It's cool," Pudge says. "I'm cool."

"Does this belong to you?" the girl asks Delia, pointing to the washer in the street next to Pudge. In the bright morning light, the machine looks sad and used up in a way it hadn't in the dim warehouse where Delia got it.

"That's right," Delia says.

"Well, I caught this guy trying to make off with it."

"Is that true, Pudge?" Delia asks. "Were you about to put this three-hundred-pound washer on your back and walk off with it?" Delia gives the girl a stare.

"But-but," the girl sputters, "the side door was standing open and . . ." She points to the chained front entrance. "I thought . . ."

The whole scene pisses Delia off. The girl's assumptions. Pudge's refusal to stand up for himself. "Pudge," Delia says without looking at him, "will you get the dolly for me?"

Once Pudge leaves, Delia expects the girl to leave, too. Instead she puts down the kickstand of her bike. "Hey," she says, looking Delia up and down, "I know who you are." She takes a few steps closer.

When the girl comes toward her, Delia recognizes the ballerina walk. Clueless, was all Calvin had said the other night when he got back from returning her boat. And clueless is what Delia thinks now. It's like the girl has no idea how she just insulted Pudge.

"You're with the hunky man," the girl says, "the one who brought my boat back."

"The hunky man is named Calvin," Delia says. Hunky man. Why can't that be enough for Delia?

"Calvin! Right."

Pudge comes back with the dolly and works the washer onto it.

"Calvin's my . . ." Delia reaches over to steady the tipped-up washer and vertigo sets the world spinning. "He's my . . ." but she can't get to the word in time. *Fiancé.* She sits down hard on the tailgate of the truck, takes a deep breath against the nausea that the spinning causes. Slowly, slowly she reaches for the edge of the tailgate and holds on to it. Tells herself there's no way she can actually fall.

"Oh, God," the girl says. "What's wrong?"

Pudge moves closer to Delia but doesn't touch her. "She's got a head injury," he says. "Makes her dizzy."

"You should take her inside," the girl tells Pudge, like she's in charge. "Let him help you inside," Bossy says, cupping Delia's shoulder and squeezing it.

Delia's not in the mood to be told what to do, but while everything's shifting around, it's too hard to say so. She reaches for Pudge's arm, and they stagger inside together.

"Sit tight," the girl says once Delia's settled onto the window seat. "Pudge and I will take care of these washers." She says it like she knows Delia. Like she knows Pudge. Like suddenly she's a part of things.

Through the big glass windows, Delia watches Pudge and the girl roll the first washer down the sidewalk toward the back of the Laundromat. By the time they come through the service door with the second one, they're best buddies. Pudge is saying, Maggie something or other, and Maggie, the girl, nods. "I know, can you believe it?" They both laugh at whatever it is they can't believe. Apparently Pudge has already gotten over the girl's rudeness. Like Calvin, Pudge is a fucking saint.

Maggie brings her canvas bag of groceries in and sets it on the window seat that runs along the front of the Bubble. Pudge lowers himself slowly onto one of the steps that lead up to the loft, which is Delia's office. His face is filled with the pain from his ruined knees, the result of an accident when he was in the Army. That's what all the beer is about. “Best pain reliever I know of,” Pudge likes to say. “And tasty, too.”

“Couple of beers in the fridge,” Delia says, checking the room for spinning. “Help yourself.”

Pudge nods to Maggie. “You want one?”

“Oh,” Maggie says, “no. I mean thanks, though.”

After he gets the beer, Pudge ducks out the back without saying good-bye, which is his habit.

“I like Pudge,” Maggie says. “He’s just really down to earth.”

“Oh, he’s down to earth all right.” The spinning has ended and with it the crabby feeling. “Pudge just looks like a mess,” she says, “but he’s a good guy.” With the crabby feeling gone, Delia can see that Maggie is maybe nicer than she first thought.

Maggie begins digging in her grocery bag, her head bent over it, the tight curls of her black hair twisting this way and that, a few of them aimed straight at heaven, completely unaffected by gravity. She’s rooting around in that bag as though sitting on this bench in the Laundromat with Delia is exactly what she planned to do with her morning. Maggie finally looks up. “Cracker Jacks?”

“What?” Delia asks, then puts her hand out to where Maggie is shaking a box of Cracker Jacks. She looks at Maggie’s mouth to see if more words will come out. Maggie has a beautiful mouth. Looking at it pushes open a door that Delia’s been keeping closed for a long, long time.

“So this is your place,” Maggie says, “your business?”

Delia nods, watches Maggie survey the rows of ragtag washers. The mismatched dryers. It must look like a dump to everyone else. Outside in front of the Laundromat, the chairs have begun to fill with people stopping to gossip on their way to the corner grocery down the block.

"It's nice sitting in here," Maggie says. "It has a really good vibe to it. You know, like soulful."

"Soulful?"

"Yeah, I don't know, it's not prefab or like a chain. It has soul."

Delia wonders if Maggie is being sarcastic. "It's all right, I guess."

"All right? Shoot. Being an entrepreneur takes *cojones*."

Cojones, Delia thinks, balls. Why does everything worth doing have to be about balls? She tells Maggie that she's saving up to go to school in the fall.

"I'm in my third year," Maggie says, then pulls the bottom of her T-shirt into a ball and knots it, exposing her tan midriff to the meager breeze of the ceiling fans. "It's completely overrated. Trust me."

A wine-colored birthmark follows the curve of Maggie's rib. It's shaped like, like Delia doesn't know what because she's trying not to stare at the private swatch of skin. It's a relief when Deysi Hernandez from down the street walks in with her old grandmother, who's pushing a grocery cart full of laundry.

"Abuelita," Delia calls out to the old grandmother, lacing her fingers together and squeezing her own hands. Abuelita nods a greeting, and Deysi searches the room for men who might want to admire her. Pudge is totally smitten with Deysi. It's a good thing he's not here to receive his usual dose of tease-and-dismiss.

Delia and Maggie watch the women fill four of the washers like it's something they're doing together, like when Delia was a kid, and she and her friends would walk down the highway to the shopping center that had a Laundromat and a dollar store. They'd go back and forth between the two, hanging out just to see what would happen. The Laundromat was always her favorite.

"You want a cold drink?" Delia finally thinks to ask. She nods toward the machine across the room. "I mean, you did save my washer from being carted off on the back of a skinny drunk man."

"Is that the going rate for good citizenship?" Maggie asks. Citizen-*she-up* is how she says it. A south Alabama accent. "You get made fun of and then somebody buys you a cold drink?"

"Looks like it," Delia says. She goes to get a couple of root beers.

When Maggie takes the drink from Delia, her long fingers seem to wrap around the bottle in slow motion, and in a very particular pattern. Like she's playing notes on an instrument. Delia holds on to the bottle a half second too long, clears her throat and goes to the back to bring change to Deysi and Abuelita, who have begun arguing over missing quarters.

From the back of the Laundromat, Maggie looks like a film star on a crappy movie set. Unlike most of the customers who frequent the Bubble, she's dressed like someone who has somewhere to go, and Delia wonders what she's doing just sitting there. Or maybe that's what college is like. You dress up and go to class every now and then, but the rest of the time you wear your nice clothes and just do whatever you want.

"Sorry," Delia says when she gets back to the window seat. "What were we talking about?"

"I just had a thought," Maggie says, slapping Delia's knee. "We're having a fish fry at the compound. You and Calvin should come." She gets up to toss the empty Cracker Jack box. On the way back, she runs her fingers across the face of the ancient snack machine left over from Big Luce's day. "Don't you just love fish fries?" Maggie asks.

As a matter of fact, Delia hates fish fries. Fish fries are the exact sort of thing she had hoped to get away from when she came to the city. That and fishing. But at least in the city, you might get invited by anyone to do just anything. Where Delia and Calvin grew up, everyone knew everyone, and it had already been decided three generations ago which people you'd invite to your house and which people you'd never get to know.

"If I could," Maggie says, sitting back down next to Delia, "I'd have a fish fry every day."

"Yeah? Well, you'll love Calvin, then."

Before Maggie leaves, it's all settled. Friday, after work, Delia and Calvin will go to the compound. Delia has heard tales from Pudge about the artists living over there, about the parties they throw, parties Delia has watched from across the bayou. What do they talk about so late at night? What will she say to them Friday when she meets them? She's no artist. According to her high school teachers, Delia has two main talents: fixing mechanical things and being a smart aleck. Neither would serve a young lady very well, the teachers said. Who you calling a lady, Delia always said back.

The night of the fish fry, Delia and Calvin cross the small bridge over the bayou and walk down a grassy path to the trailers. When they get to the compound, Maggie greets them and then there are introductions all around. The artists are mostly men, mostly pale and scrawny or chunky from inactivity. They tend to offer their area of expertise with their names. Benny Bagneris, alto sax. Calvin goes right to work having a little fun with them. "Calvin Lafleur, uncouth swain," Calvin says as he offers a permanently grease-stained hand for shaking. Calvin's not stupid, but he's not witty, either. He got that uncouth swain bit off the TV, Delia imagines. Some show with a *hey-bra* guy saying something surprising to the college folk. Unlike Delia, though, Calvin isn't much bothered by other people's assumptions. Calvin's okay with Calvin, so Calvin's okay with the world. He fits in everywhere.

"You brought wine!" Maggie says when everyone is finished laughing at the uncouth swain remark. "Fancy." Bottles of beer telescope up through the ice that has been dumped into Maggie's red canoe. Not a bottle of wine in sight. "No problem," Maggie says, "I've got a corkscrew in my trailer."

"I'll just put my beer with the rest," Calvin says and shoots Delia a told-you-so look. Earlier in the week, Delia had read that white wine goes with fish, and she went to a wine shop and asked for a nice bottle.

"Fourteen dollars?!" Calvin had turned the bottle in his hands to see if maybe there was some kind of prize floating inside.

Delia explained to him that artists weren't a bunch of bubbas who drank cheap beer. She was thinking of Maggie's expensive shoes. There would be white wine, Delia told Calvin, because it goes with fish. "White wine might go with fish," Calvin said, taking a swallow of beer and belching impressively, "but beer goes with me."

Over by the ice-filled canoe, Calvin is scoping the area for his prey of choice. "What y'all got in the way of fish?"

"Grouper," one of the guys says. "Organic." He points to a neat line of fish on a table, bought, no doubt, from one of those places that can take a week's pay and fit it into a single bag. Delia is afraid Calvin is going to laugh, but he doesn't. He just goes right over to the table and starts educating the artists about how to fillet a fish.

Maggie brings Delia to her little silver Airstream. Inside, she opens a tiny drawer in the bite-sized kitchen. "Voilà!" She hands a corkscrew to Delia.

Delia has never in her life opened a bottle of wine, but she's seen it done in movies. "What kind of artist are you?" she asks, picking at the wine's foil cap with the point of the corkscrew.

Maggie smiles. She has beautiful teeth. "The dilettante kind," she says.

Dilettante? Delia wishes she had her little notebook so she could add it to the list of words she needs to learn for college. "But like do you paint or play music or . . ."

"I write poetry," Maggie says. She winds the spirals of her hair into a tight rope and then releases it. It blooms back into a dark hurricane cloud. "But I might be changing to photography, or I might join the Peace Corps. It depends."

"On what?"

"What does anything depend on?"

This, Delia decides, is how artists are, how she herself wants to be. Everything isn't necessarily logical or practical. Life can be this way or that way or some other way altogether when you're an artist.

Maggie pulls a couple of actual wineglasses from a shelf over the sink. "What I wouldn't give to wake up with the key to a Laundromat in my pocket and know for sure that I was about to do something good with my day. Something productive."

"Trade you," Delia offers.

"You have too much life smarts. College would bore you in a minute."

Still fooling with the wine opener, Delia wonders what in the world has given Maggie the impression that she has life smarts. To her relief, the cork comes out of the bottle smoothly and with a satisfying pop. While Delia pours, Maggie crosses the small trailer to her bed, which is the only place to sit. On a small door—

a bathroom? a closet?—hangs a picture of a woman reading at a podium. Delia wants to ask about it but doesn't want to seem ignorant. It's probably somebody famous.

Maggie pats the bed. "Come. Sit. Talk."

Delia hands Maggie a glass of wine. "*Salut,*" she says and sits on the batik-printed bedspread. The spread is a sari or some other foreign word Delia can't think of right now. She's seen them in the flea market. When they toast, the glasses ring with a long, clear tone. Crystal. It dawns on her just this minute what the expression "crystal clear" means and why crystal is better than regular glass. The sound is beautiful.

Delia sits with her back to the wall, perpendicular to Maggie, whose smooth, bare legs are draped across the bed's pillows.

"So," Maggie says, taking a sip of wine, "what kind of artist are you?"

"That's one of the things I thought I might find out at college." If they'll take me, Delia wants to add. She's still not sure exactly how all that works.

Maggie pulls a book from one of the many stacks against the wall and hands it to Delia. "Have you read this?" she asks. *The Poems of Richard Wilbur.*

Delia wonders if it's a book everyone knows about, if she should know about it. She's been reading at the Laundromat, trying to get ready for college. She starts to lie and say she's read the book—she feels so far behind everyone her age—but then she wonders if maybe Maggie is going to lend it to her, which will give Delia an excuse to come back to the little Airstream.

"I haven't," Delia admits.

She's discovered that, to make Calvin fit into the picture, she's been shaving away at pieces of herself. The piece that loves to read, for instance, because Calvin is dyslexic and having books in the house just reminds him of his long struggle with school, he says. And Delia has realized that she shaved away the part of herself that deep down thinks real, true love probably has more attraction to it than what she feels for Calvin. All this redesigning has left her sleepy and dense. Shaving at herself seems like cheating or lying or some other kind of sin. Maybe it's what everyone does. Her hesitation with the wedding, her doubts, might be perfectly natural, like everyone says. But she wonders if her crankiness with Calvin might be from having to listen to the shaved pieces of herself shouting at her: *WakeUpWakeUpWakeUp.*

"Here," Maggie says, putting out her hand to take the book back from Delia. Holding the book feels good, and Delia tightens her grip, makes Maggie tug just a little before she lets go.

While Maggie flips through the poems, Delia studies a tear in the thigh of her own jeans, the ones she wore when she painted the Laundromat. When she put them on, she thought the paint spatters, the tear, looked sexy and artistic, but they could easily be mistaken for bad grooming, she sees now. The ripped fabric hangs open like an entryway to something private, and she smoothes it closed.

Maggie wags the poems in the air when she finds what she's looking for. "It's a poem about laundry," she says, "and souls." She scoots closer to Delia. The book rests easily in her hand, her long fingers spread across its back. The toes of her bare feet come to rest on Delia's thigh where Maggie pushes the denim flap open with one perfectly painted toenail.

Delia shifts away a little. The touching feels weird. Or should, she thinks. She scratches at an old scar on her forehead, the one she keeps hidden beneath her bangs.

While Maggie reads, Delia sips at the cool wine. She drifts in and out of the poem, tightening and loosening her focus until the meaning dissolves into how the letter *S* sounds moist in Maggie's mouth, the *N*'s like something. Something that makes Delia fidget. Something quick that she wants to last longer. Nnnn.

Let lovers go fresh and sweet to be undone. . . .

The way Maggie says the word *lovers* gives Delia the shivers. There are nuns in the poem—even *nuns* sounds a little dirty—and dark habits. And the mention of a difficult balance, which makes Delia think of vertigo at first. Delia crosses her legs, looks down at the chipped red paint on her own toenails. How long since she's looked at her own feet? At anyone's feet? They seem so personal, suddenly, so bare and exposed. It's like she's been on vacation from her body. She wipes her moist palms on her jeans, then takes a bigger sip of wine than she means to so that she has to hold it in her mouth and swallow a little at a time.

Outside, some hooting starts up, and the sound snaps and pops in the stillness of the trailer. Delia and Maggie both put their heads up to the small window to see what the fuss is about. Calvin is doing handstands, walking along on his palms. The scrawny artists try to copy his moves. They're already in love with him. Calvin takes the feet of Benny Alto Sax and raises them into the air, then walks the upended musician neatly over to the fire pit. The artists follow and squat around the brick-lined pit, where the fire has gone out. Calvin makes a pyramid with his hands to show the proper way to stack the wood, and the guys nod, some of them pushing on the one who must've been the architect of the faulty first attempt. City kids, Calvin's expression says.

Maggie points at Calvin. "He's a cutie, all right."

Her arm is touching Delia's while they stare out the window, their faces so, so close. "Yeah," Delia says because it's true. Everyone always thinks that Calvin is adorable. Delia misses thinking it, too.

Delia and Maggie take their wine outside and go to help with the preparations. More women have arrived. Girls, really. Next to Maggie, they all seem insubstantial, like the graphite shadow left on the page after something is erased. Delia's introduced, but she forgets the names as fast as she hears them.

Calvin commandeers a guitar, and the musicians fire up some big band music, which Calvin hates but says nothing about. Maggie grabs Delia's hand. They stutter-step out to the grass at the edge of the bayou to dance under a pale slice of moon.

It's dark now, even darker near the water. When Maggie pulls Delia into her arms, tiny fishes wiggle up Delia's spine. In the humid night air, the music bends at their backs, and they both are sweating. They spin and spin until the whole world goes dreamy, the faces around the fire blurring to a patch of warm color. Still, Delia can't stop worrying that she and Maggie will slip, will fall. The line where the ground stops and the water starts is nearly invisible in the dim light.

It's when their cheeks touch, when Delia's hand slips smoothly around Maggie's waist, that Delia begins to worry that she likes it, the touching. She begins to worry that Calvin will see it, will know. Before she can make words for what, exactly, Calvin will know, she loses the moment entirely; she can only feel a strange longing for it, a simultaneous fear of it, as though she isn't in it at all. Then the moment comes back on a sweet cloud of perfume that rushes under Delia's feet, lifting her, suspending her over the bayou, and the moon and the dancing and the longing cook themselves down to something thick and liquid inside her, and when she looks Maggie in the eye, they come this close, this close to kissing. Before they do, though (how much before? a second, maybe?), the music stops for good like that dream Delia has, the one where she's flying, and as soon as she knows it, she wakes up. Just like that, the music stops, and Calvin calls for her. "Where y'at, baby?" he hollers. "The fish is ready!"

Delia sits with Calvin on the other side of the fire from Maggie while everyone is eating their fish. When she sneaks a look through the flames, she catches Maggie looking back. They both turn their heads away then, and there's the food to compliment and the fire and the meal to enjoy. And every once in a while, the secret look.

Later that evening, out by the water, when everyone is saying their good nights, Maggie leans in and whispers something to Delia, something Delia can't make out exactly, but which her body recognizes. The mysterious words set the fishes wiggling along her spine again. Maggie pulls back after the whisper and kisses Delia on the cheek like a European, left and right and left.

Delia repeats the Euro kiss, the final part nearly landing on Maggie's mouth. Nnnn.

"Hey," Maggie says, "wait here for a second."

While she's waiting, Delia turns to look for Calvin, who's gone up on the grassy path to say good-bye to Benny Alto Sax and the others. He and a few of the guys have found a bottle of starter fluid, and they're squirting it from the path over to the fire just to watch the flames leap in the air.

Delia jumps when she feels a hand on her shoulder. She turns around to find Maggie holding out the Richard Wilbur book.

"I hope you'll come again," Maggie says.

"I hope . . ." Delia starts, but then she doesn't know how to say what she hopes. Her eyes skim past the book to Maggie's wrist and then they glide over the curve of her forearm, up to her shoulder, coming to rest at the place where a whorl of Maggie's hair dips behind a perfect ear.

Delia imagines squeezing the hurricane cloud of that hair. She feels giddy with the thought of it, with the notion that this is something she could do, that she might do. She might just wrap her fingers in Maggie's hair and then . . . what? And then kiss her, that's what. She almost says it, too. She opens her mouth as she reaches for the book of poems. "I want to . . ." but before she can form the words, vertigo makes her knees go weak, and she can feel her heart pounding in her fingertips as the world spins out from under her. She tugs at the book just a little, just enough to say yes, before she lets go. Before she lets herself fall.

If the Holy Spirit Comes for You

Dooley cradles Reet's head in the crook of his arm, and the pig's breath comes out in moist puffs that warm and then chill Dooley's face. He's not supposed to name the animals, but he does it anyway. Scooching deeper into the hay at the corner of the barn, he turns Reet's floppy head toward his little sister, T-Ya. "Feel her nose," Dooley tells her and leans across so she can reach the pig's face.

T-Ya runs two little fingers down Reet's snout. "Bawoney!" she squeals, pulling her hand away, sniffing it and then holding it to her chest. T-Ya is only three and says all kinds of things that don't make sense, so it takes Dooley a few seconds to get what she means. He touches Reet's nose, and his stomach turns. It does feel a little like baloney.

Dooley has brought T-Ya down to the barn to keep her from waking their mother so early. He wouldn't mind spending the whole day in here, but today's his thirteenth birthday, and his uncles will probably be by to get him any minute, another reason Dooley's come outside. If he stayed up in his bed, the uncles would come in and pull him right out from under the covers, and he'd be on a hunting trip before he could say, Hold up, hoss. His mama wouldn't go against them, and his daddy, their brother, is offshore. The uncles want to make his birthday special on account of his daddy being gone, and hunting is special to them. They go every Sunday morning of the season, while Dooley's aunts and cousins are at Mass.

In catechism, Dooley learned that the Holy Spirit will give you the courage to do what you need to do in life, like go hunting, for instance. Recently, though, he's begun to wonder if maybe killing is wrong, which would make hunting wrong, even if you eat what you kill. Dooley's oldest brother, who went off to the war to shoot at strangers, now lives downriver on a houseboat that he never leaves and won't let anyone visit. Every so often, Dooley meets up with him in the woods at the edge of the river. Once, he told Dooley that if you let yourself believe it's okay to kill one thing, it opens the door to killing everything. "When I kill another," his brother said, "I kill myself." That's the kind of crazy talk he came back from the war with.

"But what if the Holy Spirit tells me to go hunting?" Dooley asked. "What if the Holy Spirit says, 'Go on, Dooley. Man shall have dominion over the animals.' "

"The Holy Spirit might give you the courage to do it," his brother warned, "but God will leave you once it's done." That might be more crazy talk, but it might be true. Dooley figures if he never aims a gun at anything, he won't have to find out.

At the edge of the hay, T-Ya pushes at Reet's hindquarters. "Laps!" she says, a word she's learned from their uncles. *Baloney. Laps.* The words she uses seem random to Dooley, and he wonders how she lines them up in her mind.

"Reach me that tape," Dooley tells T-Ya, who pulls a roll of duct tape from its hiding place under an old orange crate. He wraps a neck brace he's made out of cardboard around Reet's neck and tapes it in place. Flipping two long benches onto their sides, Dooley makes a chute that's not much wider than the piglet. He hasn't told anyone about the brace and the chute, in case they don't work. He's almost positive they will, though. When he puts Reet down to walk the straight line between the benches, she staggers forward a little, banging into the sides, and then tries to back out of the chute. Dooley blocks the opening. "C'mon now, girl."

A while back, Uncle Philippe tried to talk Dooley's daddy into killing Reet. "There she goes," Philippe called out over the snuffling of the pigs, "running her laps to stay thin." Reet was a breech birth. She was the smallest, the *peeshwank,* of her litter, and she stumbled around the pen in circles, her head hanging to the side, flopping, her eyes searching back behind her for the place she meant to stop. She had trouble feeding.

"You ain't got much pig there as it is, hoss," Uncle Philippe told Dooley's daddy in his older-brother tone. "You better shoot her now while you can still get a po-boy outta the deal."

Dooley listened to Uncle Philippe's advice from the other side of the pen, watched his daddy's face to see what he might be about to do. Uncle Philippe is the oldest brother, the boss. "'As it was in the beginning, is now and ever shall be,'" Uncle Philippe is always saying. "The oldest brother is boss for life." Dooley wonders if, by the time he's grown, his oldest brother will finally leave the houseboat and get back to being the boss.

After Uncle Philippe left, Dooley's daddy didn't say another thing about Reet until just before he went offshore last week. He pulled Dooley aside in the hayloft. When his daddy's face went sad and serious, Dooley looked away. "She's miserable, son," his daddy whispered so T-Ya couldn't hear. Dooley ran his finger along a split in one of the barn's framing posts and waited for the rest to come. His daddy squeezed Dooley's shoulder. "We need to put her down."

All the other piglets had been sold, and for a whole month, it was only Reet there in the pen with Patsy, her mama. Reet wasn't miserable, Dooley knew. She just had a different approach to things. So after his daddy went offshore, Dooley made the neck brace for the piglet. He figured if he went out to the barn every morning and worked with her, he could teach her how to hold her head up and quit her circling. Probably by the time his daddy gets back, Reet will be able to show what all she learned and Dooley's daddy will see that she is a happy pig who can walk in a straight line.

In the bluish light of the lamps that hang from the barn's ceiling, T-Ya claps her hands at the end of the chute, and Reet wobbles toward her.

"Call her," Dooley says. "Say, 'C'mon, Reet, just a little more!' "

Reet trips and Dooley loops his hands under her belly and stands her up.

T-Ya pretends to fall. "Laps!" she says, landing on her back, throwing her little legs in the air.

Dooley nudges Reet, and this time she just takes off and doesn't stop until she gets to T-Ya at the end. She made it to the end twice yesterday. Three times is Dooley's goal for the day.

From outside the barn, where it's still dark, Dooley hears his uncles' three-wheelers screaming down the highway. He takes off Reet's neck brace and puts her in with her mama. "Let's go," Dooley says to T-Ya after he puts the brace and the tape under the orange crate.

They slip out of the barn and hurry down the path, past the house, and out toward the blacktop road. Four of his uncles swarm in on the oyster-shell driveway riding ATVs; Dooley's Uncle Philippe follows in his truck. The passenger door of the truck fires open right in front of Dooley, and Uncle Philippe pats the front seat.

"I can't go," Dooley says through a cloud of exhaust that grabs at his voice.

"C'mon," Uncle Philippe says. "We just going over to the back woods. Maybe get us some ducks or a couple rabbits for your birthday dinner. If we see a buck, it's all yours."

"I gotta serve at early Mass," Dooley says, "but I might can go next week." A double lie because Dooley and his mama watch Mass on TV when his daddy's offshore like he is now. And, of course, Dooley's not going to shoot anything, next week or ever.

"Father Faison took his first buck in that same woods back there," Uncle Drouet says. Meaning it's okay to skip out of serving at Mass, Dooley guesses. Father Faison will understand. It occurs to Dooley that the uncles might volunteer to call the priest and ask permission. There's no end to the trouble that lying will get you.

"Mama's sleeping," Dooley tries. "And I gotta watch T-Ya."

"We can drop T-Ya by my house," Uncle Philippe says. "Your aunt can bring her back when she comes for lunch."

"Yessir," Dooley says, "thank you, but Mama needs us here. She'll be scared if she wakes up and we're gone." Dooley leans in closer to Uncle Philippe. "Because of the baby," he whispers.

Dooley's mama lost a baby a month ago, and she's been sleeping a lot since then. And crying. Something about losing the baby makes all the men in the family keep their distance from her now. Or maybe it's the crying. Dooley can't tell. But right when he says the part about his mama needing them there, Dooley realizes it's the truth, and he waits to see if his uncles know this, too.

Uncle Drouet leans over in his ATV and pulls T-Ya onto his lap. "You want to go hunting, girl?"

T-Ya hides her face in Drouet's big camouflage jacket. Uncle Drouet puts his lips on the back of her neck and makes a fart noise and then lifts her up over his head. "Here," he says, handing her to Dooley. "We can't take this one if she's gonna fart like that."

T-Ya giggles and squirms out of Dooley's arms and then runs circles around the uncles' ATVs. Dooley wishes he was little like that and didn't have to talk.

"You coming?" Uncle Drouet asks Dooley.

"Mama said I can use my harvest money to get steaks," Dooley lies. The uncles love steak. "She's gonna take me to the Piggly Wiggly in a little bit."

Uncle Philippe makes a sound like air rushing out of a tire. "Piggly Wiggly?" He laughs until he coughs. The sound ricochets around the trees like a bullet that Dooley needs to dodge. "Why would you spend your money at the Piggly Wiggly when you got woods right there?" Uncle Philippe points into the dark in the direction of the woods that run along the edge of the bayou and out to the river, not far from where Dooley's oldest brother is sleeping on his houseboat. The sound of the guns going off in the woods will make his brother cry, Dooley knows. Or shoot back. The uncles don't seem to realize this. It's hard for them to see how other people are, Dooley guesses. People who aren't like them.

He asks the Holy Spirit for the courage to say the part about the guns and how he thinks killing is wrong. "I might can go next week," Dooley repeats, instead.

After the sun is up good, Dooley and T-Ya are on the porch outside the kitchen door when they finally hear his mama walking around inside the raised house. Dooley hopes it wasn't the sound of gunfire that woke her. "Go on and see Mama," he says to T-Ya and opens the kitchen door for her. She isn't too old for his mama to hold and whisper *good baby, sweet baby,* something his mama likes to do in the morning, when it seems to Dooley that she's the saddest.

Dooley stays out on the porch and works on the bow he's making with a yardstick and fishing line. He heard a man play a cello on TV, and the low notes pulled at the soft parts in Dooley's chest, a vibrating, good feeling. He wants to see what it sounds like if he uses a bow on his guitar. Before he gets the thing strung right, here comes the buzz of ATVs out on the blacktop, maybe half a mile away. A minute later, all five uncles come tearing down the long, oyster-shell driveway.

Uncle Philippe's big Chevy shoots in front of the ATVs and swings around to aim its tail end at the roasting pit across the driveway from Dooley. The thick smell of something freshly dead follows the truck, but Dooley doesn't see a deer anywhere. All of the uncles, dressed in crusty camouflage, scatter like dogs after rabbits, barking orders at one another. Uncle Philippe and Uncle Drouet head straight for the roasting pit, carrying a big red ice chest. When Uncle Philippe opens it, there's nothing but beer in there, and all the uncles grab one. A couple of them take their beers back to the barn, and Dooley's relieved that he remembered to take the neck brace off of Reet.

Once they've got the roasting pit set up for a fire, Uncle Philippe goes to the bed of his truck and pulls out the big green duffel that used to belong to Dooley's brother. U.S. ARMY is stenciled on the side of it. Like colored scarves from a magician's pocket, Philippe pulls a string of blue-wing teal from the bag, their shining heads flopping, white stripes like a nun's wimple around their faces. One of the ducks flaps a wing and then goes still again. Dooley watches all this from behind one of the big square posts on the side porch across the driveway, close enough to feel a part of things, but not so close that he can see the light go out of a bird's eye.

The uncles move together in a way that makes Dooley think about the inside of the clock on the mantelpiece, the one he took apart just to see what made it go. Everything inside a clock depends on everything else, and all of it has to keep moving. For days after he took it apart, Dooley couldn't pass the mantelpiece without thinking about the endlessly rocking cogs and how that quiet clock had so much movement inside it. Movement is like noise. Even when his uncles aren't talking, they seem loud to Dooley.

On the big porch, Dooley moves closer to the kitchen's screen door and watches Uncle Philippe toss the string of ducks onto the prep table next to the roasting pit. Uncle Philippe nods toward Dooley. The nod says come on and clean the ducks, but Dooley doesn't want to look at the ducks' flat eyes or yank the feathers from their wings. When Philippe pulls out the shears and the knife, Dooley turns away from his uncle to look through the screen door into the kitchen. He counts to himself, *un patate, deux patate,* waiting for his uncle to snip the filets out and scrape the organ meat into the big bucket next to his feet. Dooley will have to bring the bucket in to his mama for rice dressing, and he hopes his uncle remembers to put the lid on it. *Trois patate, quatre patate.*

Dooley is staring into the kitchen, his mind cleared by the counting, when his mama gets up from watching the TV. On the little portable set, a group of nuns is saying the rosary before Mass comes on. Dooley's mama crosses the room to the stove. All the burners are going, and cast iron pots send steamy prayers into the air, the lid of the biggest one clanging *amen* when his mama sets it down. Even with the door open, cool as it is outside, she's sweating, a moist spot like a dark hand spreading on her back. Dooley checks her face. Still sad.

Before his daddy left for the two weeks of his two-on, two-off shift, he and Dooley's mama argued. Dooley's mama doesn't want his daddy to run the supply boat out to the rigs anymore. He was offshore when she lost the baby. And now for Dooley's birthday. "You're missing all the important things," Dooley's mama said to his daddy, and she started to cry. Everything makes her cry now. "You gonna be sad," Dooley's daddy told her. "That's natural. But you gotta go on and do what you gotta do anyway. We both do. And you gotta be brave for these kids." Dooley wants to tell his mama that she doesn't have to be brave for him, that he knows how to be brave for himself, which is a lie. It seems like being thirteen is going to require a lot of lying.

There on the porch outside the kitchen door, his face mashed into the screen, Dooley watches his mama cook, her lips moving, whispering the rosary along with the TV. Suddenly the moment goes clear and sharp, like someone just adjusted an antenna inside Dooley, and he knows without a doubt that this is how he will always remember his mama. When he imagines not seeing her, having to remember her, he realizes that this moment is already gone, and he's in the next moment, one step closer to high school and then graduation and then moving away—he'll be on his own before long, and his parents will be old—and the time moving so fast in his mind makes the porch feel like it's heaving a nervous sigh under his feet.

He'd like to go in the kitchen and do something helpful for his mama, but he doesn't know what would help just now, so he stands there on the other side of the screen, near enough if she needs him, but not so close that he's in the way. He'll open the door in a minute, maybe walk across the kitchen and back through the house before Mass starts up on the TV.

The smell of blood from the ducks behind him mixes with the smell of frying onions, and Dooley's head turns all by itself just in time to see Uncle Philippe slide his knife back in the case on his belt. In the kitchen, T-Ya has fallen asleep under the table, her head resting on a stuffed Big Bird. Dooley wonders what kind of bird Big Bird is supposed to be. Long legs and a beak like a waterbird, but the wrong color. A great big yellow bird like that wouldn't last a day out on the bayou behind the house.

"Dooley," Uncle Philippe calls from behind him.

Dooley meant to go inside before his uncle finished with the ducks. He daydreams too much, his teachers say, and that's why he can't keep up with what's going on around him.

"Dooley," his uncle calls again. When Dooley turns, Uncle Philippe motions for him to come and get the carcasses.

Dooley goes over by Uncle Philippe, grabs a shovel. He wouldn't mind wearing gloves but knows better than to let his uncles catch him at it. The sun is trying to burn through a group of heavy clouds, and the light seems to go from steamy white to yellow to green right while Dooley's standing there.

"*Caw*, it smells like guts back here," Dooley says and waits for his uncle to put the limp, empty duck carcasses into the wheelbarrow.

His uncle reaches over and pinches Dooley's nose closed. "Why you breathing through your nose?"

Dooley rubs at the stink from Uncle Philippe's hand and looks down toward the bayou. There's a rainbow arched over the barn, the sky throwing a strange light on the snowy egrets poking around the cows' feet in the pasture, which has turned a blinding green in the changing light. In the opposite direction, where the bayou goes out to the river and the river out to the Gulf, clouds the color of diesel exhaust hang, a clear band of blue sky between them and the water. Dooley watches the dark clouds drift and pile up behind the bare cypress trees. When he looks back at the barn for the rainbow, it disappears while he's watching, but then it's there again, so that Dooley isn't sure what he sees and what he doesn't.

The wheelbarrow is heavy and hard to maneuver. Dooley has to shift his weight down and bow over his load to keep from losing control. He finds himself looking right into the blank eye of an empty, wingless duck whose insides have been scooped out. Its neck is flopped back, its chest hollowed and flat, the whole bird folded like a thick sweater.

When Dooley gets to the garbage pit, he tosses some brush in and then shovels the carcasses. *Un patate, deux patate,* he goes out the secret door of the counting, away from duck heads and feet, flopping, empty. Steam rises from the still-warm parts. Dooley quickly looks away. He knows that the ducks are dead, that they can't feel anything now. Still, he'd rather not have to put them in a hole, would rather not cover their faces with brush and send their bodies out of this world on a flame. The baby his mother lost is in a hole in the cemetery down the road, a tiny little headstone marking the spot where his whole family shoveled dirt on top of her. Sometimes Dooley dreams that she opens her eyes down there in the dark. When he has that dream, there's no amount of counting that can get the picture out of his head.

Dooley throws some more brush in the pit and douses the whole thing with starter fluid. Fire rushes up toward his hand almost before he drops the match. The burning duck fat smells good. Dooley wishes he didn't like it so much.

He glances out in the direction of the Gulf where his daddy is working, but not the Gulf where his brother went to war. Dooley's never going to work on the rigs or go to war, either one. He's going to go to New Orleans like his older sister, Delia, and her fiancé. In the city, people get their dinner from a store, and you can stand on a street corner and play guitar for money. Sometimes Dooley can just see it all, how everything is there waiting for him, and he wishes he could fast-forward himself into his future.

The dark clouds out over the water make a sad music percolate up in Dooley, and he whistles the notes as he walks back along the path to the house. The minor and seventh chords in his head pull at his heart, like when the soloist at Mass sings "Ave Maria." Dooley can tell that whoever wrote that song knew about the lonely feeling he gets sometimes.

Over in the grassy area between the roasting pit and the barn, Philippe and the other uncles have left off tending the fire and started a game of touch football. Dooley watches his uncles crouch and run, watches touch turn to tackle, while he hoses out the wheelbarrow. The cows press themselves against the back fence and watch the game with their moist, worried eyes. On the other side of the fence, the egrets comfort their big friends. Here cow, here now, Dooley imagines the birds saying. Everything is fine.

Back up on the porch, Dooley peeks inside through the kitchen door screen. His mama has gotten the bucket of organ meat herself, and now she's watching Mass on TV while T-Ya plays a toy xylophone at her feet. His mama picks his sister up and shows her how to cross herself.

"Dooley," his mama calls out to the porch, kneeling as the congregation on TV kneels in their pews, "you helping your uncles?"

Dooley had forgotten his mama could see him there on the other side of the screen. "Yes, ma'am," he tells her. "I'm helping."

His mama turns back to the Mass. In the name of the Father and the Son and the Holy Spirit, the priest says on TV, and Dooley crosses himself and hopes that God understands about the lies he told his uncles this morning. He tries to remember how Father Faison explained the Holy Spirit, but can't. It's supposed to be inside you, but that doesn't seem right. In Dooley's mind, the Holy Spirit always seems like clouds. Like storm clouds that come for you and toss you into some other life by telling you what you're meant to do. When God told Abraham to sacrifice his son, Abraham tied his own boy up on top of some kindling because the Holy Spirit came to him and told him to be strong, to have faith. The Holy Spirit can whisper whatever It wants, whether it makes any sense or not, and you've got to do it. If you don't, it's the same as telling God you don't trust Him. Be brave and kill a deer. Shoot a stranger for wearing the wrong uniform. Set your son on fire. It doesn't make a lick of sense to Dooley. The Holy Spirit seems like a troublemaker. Anyone would know that Abraham, like Dooley's brother, must've lost his mind once he realized what he'd let the Holy Spirit talk him into. Dooley knows he isn't ready, will never be ready, to do the kinds of things the Holy Spirit will ask.

"T-boy," one of Dooley's uncles calls to him. "Come on, we need one more."

Dooley turns away from the kitchen door and looks out at his uncles.

"Think fast," Uncle Drouet yells from out on the grass and shoots the football in a blazing spiral all the way up to the porch.

When Dooley catches it, he jams a couple of fingers on his right hand. He does his best to throw the ball back, but it falls short. Dooley's been practicing his passing with his daddy. And he's strong from lifting milk cans. He's a pretty good passer. But for the way his uncles play, passing isn't enough. Dooley avoids these games when he can.

"Time out!" Uncle Philippe calls. He reaches into the ice chest they've dragged out into the grass, fishing for another beer. He pops the top and goes over to poke at the fire.

Dooley gets down off the porch to get a better look. His uncles—his daddy, too—are very particular about their fires, and Dooley watches how Uncle Philippe pokes it just enough so air can get in, but not so much that it won't burn evenly.

Uncle Philippe is sweating in the cool air, out of breath from the game. He hands Dooley the poker. "Push that big log till it's almost straight up."

Dooley does as he's told while Uncle Philippe watches.

"Looks good," Philippe says about Dooley's arrangement of the logs. "You 'bout to put me outta business." Dooley sniffs and nods, looks for other logs that need poking.

Uncle Philippe goes back into the shed. "T-boy," he calls out to Dooley, "give that fire a little more air, huh?"

When Uncle Philippe comes back, he's carrying a flat grilling cage, the small one, the one they use for *cochon du lait.* Dooley means to ask why, but here comes the football right at him, and he drops the poker. The ball drills into his skinny chest before he can get his hands up to stop it.

In the distance, dark clouds are piling up over the Gulf, their weight pushing the bright strip of blue sky into the water. If Dooley closes one eye, the rainbow, which has appeared again over the barn, looks like it's spraying up out of his Uncle Drouet's head. Like a thought that you can see and then not.

Dooley leaves the roasting pit and trots out to stand next to Drouet, who has kicked off his hunting boots and now is playing in his socks. Don't move, Dooley wants to say to his uncle. Your head is a pot of gold. Just when Dooley is getting used to the rhythm of the game, his Uncle Philippe butts into him—*C'est ça, tête dur!*—and knocks him on his ass. *Tête dur*, hard head. I wish, Dooley thinks, rubbing the spot where his head hit one of Uncle Drouet's boots when he fell. On the next snap, Dooley fires out of the line and circles behind Uncle Philippe, keeping low to the ground, waiting. Uncle Philippe moves back and back until he finally trips over Dooley. *Fump!* His uncle goes down like he's been shot. Knowing where to stop, Dooley has learned, is just as important as knowing where to go.

"*Caw*," his uncle says, sitting up in the grass, smiling, "look at the *peeshwank*."

By the time the game ends, it hurts when Dooley takes a deep breath, but he doesn't complain. Uncle Drouet puts him up on his shoulder and runs a victory lap around the fire with him. All the uncles grab a beer, and Dooley gets to have some, to show he's not a *peeshwank*.

The uncles drink and poke at the fire, which is going pretty good now. It's getting on close to noon, and Dooley remembers the steaks. He doesn't want to get caught in that lie. "Can somebody take me to the store?"

The uncles look at each other and just for a second they all stop moving at once.

Dooley feels something tighten inside him. "It's almost time to start cooking, huh?"

"Yeah," Philippe says, "it's about time, I guess." He rocks out of his chair and slaps his thighs.

Everyone looks at the barn, and the hair on Dooley's neck stands up.

Uncle Philippe darts around the fire and heads right for Dooley, scooping him up before Dooley has a chance to run inside. "Free swats!" all the uncles whoop. Philippe flips Dooley over his shoulder and carries him all the way back to the barn, the other uncles swatting at Dooley's butt, once for each birthday. On the back side of the barn is a slaughter pen, and Uncle Philippe sets Dooley down next to it. Reet's in the pen, running frantic circles, her head tipped to one side, her ears up, eyes searching for Patsy, her mother.

The reason for the roasting cage and Dooley's part in it becomes clear, and, too late, he turns to run back toward the house. He's surrounded by uncles.

"You gonna do fine," Uncle Drouet says. When Dooley tries to back up, Drouet puts his hand on Dooley's shoulder, not pushing, but not moving aside, either.

The ground feels like it's pitching, like a boat on water, so that Dooley has to grab at something to keep from falling. He leans into Uncle Philippe, who's come alongside him. "She ain't never gonna be right, hoss," his uncle says.

Dooley wonders if such a thing could possibly be true. It seems that if it was true, then everyone would believe the same thing. There's only one truth, is what Dooley has always thought. "She is too gonna be right," Dooley says to the ground, careful to keep his eyes off of Reet. "She just needs some time."

Uncle Drouet's hand tightens on Dooley's shoulder. "C'mon, now," he says, quieter than Dooley has ever heard him say anything. Uncle Philippe guides Dooley into the small pen with Reet;

the other uncles stand along the edges. Dooley knows there's no turning back. If he refuses, one of the uncles will do what he won't. Dooley tries to think out whether he'd rather be killed by someone he knows or by a stranger.

"Slipknot," one of the uncles says, handing Dooley some rope. Dooley kneels in the dirt with Reet, and she stops her circling and noses at him, smells something wrong and goes back to circling again. Dooley makes a slipknot with his stiff, jammed fingers. He fumbles around a little and then loops the slipknot over Reet's back legs, binds back and front legs together, away from her neck. The dark cloud of the Holy Spirit hovers over the pen and gives Dooley Its awful command.

"Don't be such a *duh-doot*," his uncles holler when Dooley starts to cry. He's past caring who sees him cry, though.

This *cochon du lait* in front of him was Reet this morning, her neck getting stronger, her eyes straight ahead in the little walking chute. She flops her head back into Dooley's chest now, and he pulls her up next to his face, puts his arms around her, runs one hand down her smooth snout. He sees stars blinking in the dark clouds over him and realizes he's forgotten to breathe.

"Good pig," he says to Reet, who is a baby, the way T-Ya is a baby, who still needs her mother. "Sweet pig," he says, rocking her. A group of egrets flies over the pen, brightens the sky for a few seconds and then disappears. "Everything is fine," Dooley lies. Reet yelps, and Patsy answers from the barn where she's throwing herself against the door trying to get out. The noise cuts right through Dooley.

Uncle Philippe gives Dooley the knife. "Make sure you hit it right the first time, now," he says, "or she's gon' suffer."

Dooley's seen the suffering. Seen pigs chased for sport before the cut is made, so that when the knife finally goes in, the storm in the animal's pounding heart empties in a quick, bright shower, everyone cheering, even when they mean to scream. Or cry. Dooley wishes his daddy was here, wonders if he knows about this. Wonders if he's maybe planned this with the uncles, a question Dooley will never, never ask.

His hand does what the Holy Spirit requires, but Dooley doesn't watch. *Un patate, deux patate.* He sits with Reet's back against his chest. He pulls her floppy head up, cradling it in the crook of his arm, clearing a path for the knife, his leg braced over Reet's bound legs. Dooley knows it's wrong to sit this way, to aim the knife back toward his own body, but if the sharp blade slips from Reet's throat, if Dooley stabs himself in the process, he was only doing what the Holy Spirit asked. He holds Reet to his chest and makes himself go still inside so she doesn't have to feel his scared feelings.

It's some other boy and some other hand pushing the point of the knife in, slitting Reet's throat. *Trois patate, quatre patate,* Reet's body jerks a little and then goes still. That same strange boy hangs Reet upside down on the hook at the back of the barn, a dark world puddling on the ground beneath her. The uncles slap the boy's back and say excited things. *Dooley . . .* they say. *Dooley . . .*

The real Dooley opens and closes his bloody hands, concentrates entirely on the sticky sound. The real Dooley stands looking off toward the bayou, not at the dark diesel clouds, which have filled the afternoon sky completely, but at a constellation of snowy egrets perched in the bare cypress trees, watching, quiet, still.

Issue Is

The courtyard is crowded with locals, the humidity and the stench of a hundred-year-old sewer leak having kept all the tourists in the main building of the bistro. Delia's table is snugged into the curved corner at the base of a winding stair. Across from the stairs is a storeroom that houses the overstock of beer and wine and olive salad, a room entered frequently by waiters who mostly emerge empty-handed, the smell of pot chuffing from their clothes. Delia loves the Napoleon House. It's where she and Maggie had their first official date. And she loves this corner table with its unobstructed view of the whole patio. It's *their* table.

She adjusts the straps on her new sandals and knows for certain that it was a mistake to wear them. They were a gift from Maggie, who has just gotten back from a business trip to Vancouver, home to the international chain of high-end coffee shops for which she is an executive. This afternoon when Delia pulled the slingbacks from their delicate nest of tissue, she found a card tucked at the bottom of the box. "M.," the card said, "it was lovely as always, and you're lovely. Think of me when you wear these in that hot town of yours." Several *X*'s and *O*'s. No signature. Delia slipped the card in the pocket of her blouse, right over her heart, and began to wait for the moment when she would have to ask Maggie about it.

This morning, they stayed in bed late, filling the room with sharp, shining incantations: the *ohh* and *ohh* and *you-you-you* of first-day-back sex. Later, Maggie made grits and *grillades.* When Delia pulled the coffee from the stove to pour it, that's when Maggie handed her the shoebox with a flourish, with flowers from their garden, with a *Slingbacks pour vous!* followed by a story about how, between meetings, she'd spent some time shopping. She sealed the lie with a kiss on Delia's mouth. It's exactly the sort of moment and exactly the sort of lie that Delia has recently feared would be the end of them.

"Baby love!" Maggie chirps at Delia now, crossing the courtyard after a trip to the primitive bathroom, an awful room that requires a snaky trek through the bistro's kitchen. Delia admires Maggie's grace, her posture, her loose-hipped, duck-footed gait with its remnant of ballet lessons in it.

When she sits, Maggie tucks a long, muscled leg beneath herself. "This just in," she says. "Brandi now hearts Jason *in plaid pants, dude.*" Maggie often doctors the pedestrian sentiments she finds on the bathroom wall by adding even more hackneyed phrases to them. She won't put up with trite graffiti. "It's an assault on the public, right?" From behind one ear she pulls a brown eyebrow pencil and sets it on the table next to a bowl of olives.

They have always written on the bathroom wall here with an eyebrow pencil. Song lyrics with double meanings—*If I said you had a beautiful body would you hold it against me?*—and lists of items that should be banned: plaid pants, *dude.*

Delia tries to catch the eye of their waiter, Sal, who, with the other waiters, stands leaning against the far wall next to a cigarette machine. She's thirsty and anxious to give her senses a soaking.

"Aren't you going in?" Maggie tips her head in the direction of the bathroom. "Don't you want to write something?"

"Not yet," Delia says. Her heart tries to engage, slips gears and fails. She looks across the courtyard at Sal and shows him her thirstiest face. He pushes himself off the wall with the bottom of his foot and trundles over.

"Maggie, Delia, how are you?" They've known Sal for every one of the ten years he's worked there. He's *their* waiter.

"We're good," Maggie answers without looking at Delia and then asks after Sal.

"Sweetheart, I'm in love," Sal says, swooning. "I'm just all aquiver."

Delia gives him a smile. Sal falls in "love" easily and a lot. As though love enters through the openings of the body.

"Pimm's Cup?" Sal asks.

"No, honey," Delia says, scooting her chair back and crossing her legs. "We'd like a couple of beers. Abita, please. Or," Delia turns to Maggie, "maybe you want something else? Something *different*?"

"I'll have a beer if you're having one." Maggie digs first in her own purse and then in Delia's until she finds a nail file. She files her nails the way some people smoke, reflexively and excessively.

Delia flips her sunglasses up on top of her head, squeezes one eye shut against the midafternoon glare and trains the other eye on Maggie, waiting.

They've rescheduled this outing twice now, its ostensible purpose to coordinate their busy schedules, to find a way to spend more leisure time together, a suggestion from the therapist they've been seeing. It seems really artificial to Delia that they should have to plan their leisure time, but she knows something has to give. May already have given.

"Hey, how did Dooley's move go?" Maggie asks, shifting in her chair, sliding the bowl of olives left, then right, then left again.

Delia's brother, Dooley, had been living with them so he could put all his money into getting his band off the ground. Moving out was a pretty big deal, a milestone, and one more item to add to the long list of things Maggie has missed because of all the traveling she has to do for work. Her concern for Dooley is genuine, but it's expressed here, at least in part, in an effort to divert the attention she senses Delia is about to aim at her. Maggie's debutante background has made her a genius at sidestepping unpleasant conversation.

"Dooley's move went fine. He made me freeze you some cake from the housewarming." Dooley adores Maggie.

"Mmm. Cake." Maggie nudges Delia's leg. "And you? What's new with you?"

Delia recrosses her legs. "I'm not sure I know the answer to that one." The slingback on her foot swings, tick-tock, tick-tock, a timer running down, a shoe bomb about to go off. "You ready to schedule some leisure time?"

"Can we do it later," Maggie asks, "like after we're dead?" She leans forward and drops the nail file back in Delia's purse, then tucks her short green skirt beneath herself.

"Now is later," Delia says. She's not crazy about the stupid therapy assignments, either. Their therapist said they need to work on getting their priorities in order. "What if her priorities are screwed up?" Delia asked Maggie after they got that piece of advice. "What if a month from now she quits being a therapist and goes out to the woods to be a forest ranger so she doesn't have to talk to anyone? What if when people ask her, she says, 'I never should've been a therapist. I had my head up my ass the whole time.' What if she says that?"

And now they're scheduling leisure time. Delia's not sure how much good it will do since most of their leisure time is spent catching up on things that are already over. It's always the same. Before they get a chance to work out what they've been bickering about, Maggie has to leave. The whole thing makes Delia long for the sort of marriage her parents' generation had. Or Delia's idea of it, anyway. No poking, no probing, no therapy. It required a lot of Valium, Delia guesses, but what doesn't?

Maggie extracts her PDA from deep in her gigantic purse. Unlike an affair with another woman, whom Delia neither knows nor has to see, Maggie's affair with her PDA is right in Delia's face. Not in their bed, exactly, but never far from it. Delia hisses at the evil little intruder.

Maggie holds up the PDA and displays it like a spokesmodel. See? the gesture says. I'm doing my part. She plucks the stylus from its holder to show that she's ready, that she's taking this seriously.

There's no sign of guilt on Maggie's face, only a distracted smile, an expression that so captures Maggie's essence that Delia thinks of it as belonging to a painting, *Maggie at Rest.* It's that very look that makes Delia question her interpretation of the card she found at the bottom of the shoebox this afternoon. She's been trying to talk herself into thinking that maybe the shoes were an innocent gift from a business associate, that, at worst, Maggie is guilty of being a romantic hack for trying to pass them off as a thoughtful present she picked out just for Delia. And are shoes really a sexy kind of gift? Delia supposes that they are for Maggie, who is the Imelda Marcos of the lesbian community.

Sal is leaning against the wall again, and Delia watches Maggie turn her hands up to show him they hold no drink. The waiter slaps his palm to his forehead and rushes to the bar.

"We don't have to do this," Delia says. "Not if you think it won't do any good." Delia's tired. The idea of giving up takes hold in her mind.

Maggie squints into her PDA, taps screen after screen of Delia doesn't know what. "Look at this," she says, holding out the device for Delia to see. There's a picture of the two of them from some Mardi Gras past. Arm in arm, they lean against the window of the Laundromat that Delia owns, the sidewalk in front of them dark except for the glow from the snack machine inside. The cardboard hands of *The Scream* are clamped over Delia's ears, and her eyes are painted wide with shock, her mouth circled in black, a fixed O of horror. Next to her, Maggie is draped in bright multicolored streamers, a birthday cake for a hat. Delia wants to ask how this picture came to be on the PDA. And why. But she knows that she'll doubt every explanation that points to love. The words might still be true, but maybe not in the way Delia has thought.

She fishes around in her wavy hair, which the humidity has tightened into curls, hooks a ringlet and pulls on it until it's straight, then throws it back. Delia wishes Sal would come with the drinks so she can get herself to an easier, if not a better, place. It would be nice to spend an afternoon drinking and reciting bawdy poems—*There was a gay man from Khartoum*—or indulging in prattle as they used to in the early years, when Delia's Laundromat was still new and Maggie spent her time changing majors at the rich kids' college Uptown. In retrospect it seems like a simpler time, though Delia knows it was just a different kind of complicated. She decides to keep the card hidden awhile longer, to give Maggie the chance to bring up the real source of the shoes, to say something, anything, about the maker of the *X*'s and *O*'s.

"Delia," Maggie says, from what seems a great distance. "The shoes. You're ruining your new shoes."

Delia looks down at her foot. She's been smacking the delicate leather of the slingback against the leg of Maggie's chair. "Where'd you say you got these?" Delia asks.

"There are so many new shops on Robson," Maggie says. "You should see."

"But these particular shoes . . . ?"

"We went a lot of places . . ." Maggie says and stops herself. "I can't remember, sweetie. Robson Street somewhere, I guess."

After a minute, Maggie reaches down to stop Delia's foot, which has begun kicking again. While she's down there, she adjusts the sugar packets that have been tucked under the feet of their table to keep it steady.

"I wonder if there's much lead in all that crumbling paint," Maggie muses, sitting up. She points at the flaking paint on the curved walls of the historic staircase, taking Delia's eyes up and away from the shoes. "It could fall in our drinks," Maggie says, "and then we'd have to ride the special bus to school."

Delia catches sight of a bruise stamped on Maggie's calf, the size and shape and color of a dark pansy. When did it happen? How? A comma of hair keeps sneaking away from its home behind Delia's ear and sticking to her cheek. She loops it back into place, then runs one finger over the large scar beneath her bangs, the wrinkled remains of a childhood injury that itches when she's upset.

Waiting for words, true words, any words, Delia tries offering her leg for touching. She watches her own calf, watches Maggie's bare toe rise and fall along it, but can't feel the simple animal comfort of it. She wants Maggie to confess without being asked, or to say, "Gay Steve from Seattle gave me those. He got a pair for himself, too."

"Do you think that's what's made Sal so spacey?" Maggie asks. "All that crumbling lead paint?"

"Could be," Delia sighs. "Probably other things, too, though." She juts her chin toward the bar where Sal is chatting up a fireman. Delia stares hard at him. Sal finally turns back toward the courtyard and holds up one finger to show that their drinks are on the way.

The sound of Ella Fitzgerald warbling on a scratchy LP—a song about birds and bees and doing it—fills the patio. It was the first thing Maggie ever wrote on the bathroom wall with eyebrow pencil, an invitation she'd sent Delia in to read. *Let's do it; let's fall in love,* Maggie wrote that night several months after they'd begun dating, after they'd gotten up, unsteady and oblivious to the other patrons, and danced to the song right there in the courtyard of the Napoleon House. Like a dream. Like Delia and Maggie when they were new.

Under the table, Delia taps her feet to the music. The smack of the slingbacks' expensive soles on the brick is high-pitched and hollow, like the disapproving click of a tongue. She imagines that Maggie has planned this, has probably tipped Sal to play the song so that they can dance. As though they can waltz away their troubles, dip and glide across this rocky time, back to their sure beginnings. Delia closes her eyes, lets the moment pass in silence.

At last Sal comes with their drinks somewhere toward the end of the painfully long song. "Two Pimm's Cups," he says, and without another word, he pivots toward his wall and leaves them.

Delia watches Maggie pick up her drink and chase a cucumber slice around in its pool of alcohol. Before she can get the fruit to her mouth, it slides from between her fingers and slaps wetly onto the bricks beneath the table.

When Maggie attempts a dive for the cucumber in Delia's glass, Delia covers it with her hand. "Oh, no, uhn-uh."

"You wanted these all along, didn't you?"

"I did want them," Delia says. Getting a Pimm's Cup without actually ordering it is something of a sport for them.

Maggie sighs. "Such a clever girl."

There's real admiration in her voice, and for a few seconds, Delia is buoyed by it, by the respect they have always had for each other. This could be a lie, too, though—an illusion—couldn't it? Delia feels herself tear up and pulls her sunglasses down for cover. Like a two-year-old, she often cries when she's confused. Or when she means to be angry. The crying only makes her angrier, which leads to more tears.

Maggie picks up the eyebrow pencil. She taps out a little song against their glasses. "Aren't you going to write something?"

"I am," Delia says, "but later."

Maggie continues tapping her deedly-deedly-doo on the glasses. "Now is later, I think is what you said before."

Delia takes a deep breath and pushes it out between her closed lips. She reaches down and sticks her finger between the slingback and her Achilles tendon. The strap is cutting into her, and so is the tapping, the pretend-innocent song, the deedly-deedly-doo. Delia jerks the eyebrow pencil out of Maggie's hand and uses it to stretch the strap of the shoe. Someone, somewhere knows about Maggie's fetish for slingbacks. Delia presses her lips together, hard. She holds up two fingers for Sal, and, to her relief, he goes directly to the bar. She slows her breathing, weighs her next move. Once she pulls the card out, there'll be no turning back.

They started therapy six months ago because Maggie was traveling so much for work, and she was feeling stressed by it. Or because Delia felt alone in their relationship. Or because, like everyone who's been together for any amount of time, they'd simply stopped talking about what they hoped to do and took care of what they had to do. The constant present tense of their lives was wearing them out, making them bicker.

The therapist said that their relationship was "do" heavy, that they needed to spend less time doing and more time being. They needed to talk more, to participate in the process, she said. They'd both laughed at that, at the word *process*. But behind the therapist's back, of course.

"We got issues, missy," Maggie said in the car after their first session.

"But only the one," Delia acknowledged. "Issue is or issue ain't my baby."

Later that evening, Delia had howled with laughter when Maggie grabbed her and said, "Come on and let me *process* this," and smacked Delia's ass.

For all the fun they made of therapy, though, Delia thought it was helping. They were arguing less. And if phone sex counted, they were talking more. But now the shoes, the card.

Across the table, Maggie pokes at her PDA, flipping through the electronic calendar. She stares into the tiny screen like it's a crystal ball. "When are we going to the beach?" she asks the device, then looks up at Delia. "Everything is always so nice at the beach."

Maggie leans back in her chair, closes her eyes and smiles as though she's already there, the sugary sand beneath her, cocktails at the ready and the Gulf heaving happy sighs at her feet. "So?" Maggie asks, opening her eyes slowly and staring first into her PDA and then right at Delia.

Delia flinches from the eye contact. The beach. What if they could go to the beach and have a good time? What if they could come back refreshed, renewed, and leave the stranger's *X*'s and *O*'s buried in the sand? "I reckon we might end up at the beach," she says.

Her beloved's expression softens into a look that Delia would like to think Maggie reserves just for her. "I like it when you say 'I reckon.' Say it again."

Delia tries to imagine that they are strong enough to get past this, to figure out a way. She should just tell Maggie about finding the card, just put it out there.

"I want for us to go together," Maggie says. "Not just have a few overlapping days, but really go together this time."

"We might be able to do that."

"If we talk," Maggie says.

"If we *make a plan for our leisure time*," Delia says, mocking their therapist.

"If we participate in the *process*, you mean."

"Process this!" they say together because now it's what they always say when someone uses the word *process*. For a few seconds, Delia knows why she and Maggie are together. Knows why she can't just quit. Then the clarity leaches back into wherever it came from.

"And what about our anniversary?" Maggie asks. "We should have a party. Like a really big one."

Delia rolls her eyes. "I'd rather go to the beach." Last year they didn't make it to the beach at all. Maggie had gotten a promotion, and the traveling had started. And then it was just too hard to plan anything. One evening, though, when Delia came home from work, their tiny backyard had been made into a beach. Maggie had hung colored lanterns—Delia loves colored lanterns—and made elaborate, fruity cocktails. Don Ho sang on the stereo.

Until this very afternoon, Delia has always been sure of Maggie's love, of her attention. She tries to get at that certainty now, to believe that nothing's really changed. That the welded joint of love is strong and will hold.

When she looks across the courtyard, it's just in time to track Sal's slow approach to their table. He sets down two more Pimm's Cups. This second round is even stronger than the first, Sal's compensation, Delia knows, for taking so long. They cut each other slack. They make allowances, and it all evens out. Like now. The alcohol has begun to loosen the tightness inside Delia. She watches Maggie, pecking things into her PDA, stopping to tap the stylus against the drum of her cheek, whose skin is stretched taut, her mouth opening and closing to make a happy little tune.

They drink quietly for a while, both staring across the courtyard where a very drunk man, a tourist festooned with out-of-season Mardi Gras beads, is trying to buy cigarettes from the machine. He puts money in and pulls on the knob. When nothing happens, he puts in more money and then more. The machine is broken. There's a sign that says as much. But the man wants what he wants. "Connect the dots, why don't you," Delia says in his direction.

For ten, maybe fifteen minutes more, Delia and Maggie listen to *The Barber of Seville*, which is an old part of the Napoleon House's extensive opera collection. Sal brings another round of drinks to the table without being asked. "Ladies," he says with a crisp flourish of his drink tray and walks off. He leaves the empty glasses, which have begun to sweat. Cool drops of water drip through the mesh of the table onto Delia's bare legs. The drops cling to her skin and slide down around her ankles, moistening the leather straps of the slingbacks, which are digging into Delia's heels.

Maggie takes a long drink. "These are good, aren't they," she coos. When Delia doesn't say anything, Maggie looks into her eyes. "Are we playing Guess Why I'm Mad?"

"We might be."

Maggie pulls the cucumber from Delia's drink. When Delia reaches for the stolen fruit, Maggie holds it away. A wave of anger washes over her, and tears start at the corners of her eyes.

"Close your eyes," Maggie says.

"Why?"

"Trust me, will you?"

Delia feels Maggie lift her sunglasses and set slices of cucumber on her closed eyelids. It feels great. The cool blackness, the nothingness, is a little vacation from the moment, and Delia's relieved to have it. Too quickly, the cucumbers take on her heat, and she sets them on the plate of olives.

Her feet have begun to swell from the sitting and the hot day and the alcohol, and Delia tries to adjust the straps of the slingbacks again. Out of the corner of her eye, she watches Maggie watching her.

"These shoes are hurting me," Delia says.

Maggie is looking right at Delia's feet now, and she's nervous, Delia sees.

"They're hurting you. I'm sorry."

"They're cutting into me."

"I said I'm sorry. Here, let me take them back. You can have mine." Maggie removes her designer flip-flops and offers them to Delia.

"I think I already have your shoes, don't I?" Delia says. She nearly tears her pocket trying to get at the card, whose *X*'s and *O*'s she slaps on the table between them.

Maggie puffs her cheeks, which is what she does when she doesn't want to cry. She shakes her head no, no, no, and then digs in her purse—for an explanation, maybe?—but comes up empty-handed. She funnels ice into her mouth, chews loudly.

Delia thumbs an olive into the air for something to do, catches it neatly in her mouth, then bites down on the hard core in an attempt to *feel the anger,* another assignment from therapy. She scrapes off the salty meat with her teeth, then spits the pit into her palm and closes her hand, making a fist around the sharp little point. Neither of them says anything for what seems a long, long time.

Delia flicks the olive pit in Maggie's direction, missing her by enough to make it seem accidental. Then she winds her hair into a French twist and anchors it with the eyebrow pencil. "I'm going to the bathroom," she says, gesturing toward the kitchen behind Maggie. She buses the table for Sal, scissoring, with one hand, the empty drink glasses, and scoots past Maggie.

Without getting up, Maggie reaches behind herself and grabs Delia's wrist, pulls it to her cheek. Kisses it with a tenderness that fires up Delia's heart, makes it catch, its gears engage. The back of Maggie's neck looks vulnerable beneath her chic haircut where the skin has begun to crease with age and her refusal to use sunblock.

It was so smooth when they first started out. Maggie turns in her chair and looks up at Delia. She puffs her cheeks against the tears. "I shouldn't have accepted the shoes. I shouldn't have . . . I messed up. I messed up, Delia."

Delia can feel Maggie's hand shaking, or maybe it's her own, and it makes her want to comfort Maggie or kill her, though she can't tell which. Most of all, though, Delia wants to say the thing she's just now remembered. She wants to say how, years ago, at a New Year's Eve party, which was right up the historical staircase of this exact bistro, Delia made out with a woman she knew who was visiting from out of town. They were both drunk, everyone was, and they had begun flirting while they waited in the long, long bathroom line. When the door finally opened, they entered together and went directly to kissing. Why? Delia still doesn't know. They would've done more had there not been threats from the squirming line outside.

In the cab on the way home from the party, Delia had started her confession. "I messed up . . ." she said.

Giggling from all the champagne, Maggie grabbed Delia's wrist and kissed it. "Uh-oh," she said. "What'd you do, girl?"

But then Delia thought it didn't make any difference what she'd done. It was a stupid New Year's Eve kind of thing. She put her mouth on someone else. They had a moment. Big deal. She loved Maggie. By the time they got in the cab that night, it was already in the past, and they were driving away from it. Delia let the subject drop.

Crossing the courtyard, Delia catches sight of Sal inside mooning over a delivery man. She holds up the glasses to show him that she's cleared the table, and he turns away from his conversation to blow her a kiss. It all seems so normal.

In the bistro's kitchen, Delia adds their glasses to a line of dirty dishes waiting near the sink. A rack, fresh from the dishwasher, steams at the counter's edge, lipstick persevering on several cups. One of them has been filled with a perfect cappuccino and forgotten. Probably by Sal. A neat disc of foam rises above the carmine crescent where a stranger's lips have left their mark. Delia reaches instinctively to clear the stain. It happens, she thinks, pulling her hand away. It happens all the time. She turns from the cup, from the steaming rack, the sink, and makes her way to the bathroom door, which sticks just a little before it opens.

Titty Baby

"You got titties," Jerry Beatty told Pudge in P.E. this afternoon. Right in front of everyone. The entire fifth grade had to run the fifty-yard dash, and Pudge was last. He always is. When he got close to the finish line, a bunch of Jerry's friends threw themselves on the ground and covered their heads. "*Incoming!*" they yelled, like soldiers on TV.

Now Pudge cuts down Palmyra Street away from the rest of the after-school crowd. Every once in a while, he moves his notebook aside to study his problem chest. There's something about his new shirt that shows off his titties, which, up until today, were a kind of secret. His mother bought him this new outfit. For incentive, she said. It's not for him, exactly, but for the slim boy he's meant to be.

"Big Luce!" Pudge calls down the street. Big Luce is about to walk back inside the Corner Laundry, and Pudge wants to catch her before she does. His tight pants cut into his thighs, and walking fast turns up the volume of the new denim scratching against itself. *Stampede!* he hears in his head when he tries to run. And the laughing. "Big Luce!" Pudge calls again and waves.

Big Luce stops at the gate behind the Laundromat. "How goes it with you?" she asks as Pudge pushes straight into the courtyard, where his classmates won't be able to see him.

Pudge's insides are fizzing, but he can't think of what that's called. Fizzing. I'm fizzing, he tries out in his mind. "Okay, I guess," he says to Big Luce.

"That bad, huh?"

It might be that Big Luce can read his mind. Or maybe she's kidding? Sometimes people are kidding, but Pudge doesn't catch on in time. Or maybe she saw the titties poking out of his new shirt this morning and knows what kind of day they got him. His Aunt Alma will be coming through the gate soon, and Pudge wants to tell Big Luce about the titty problem before his aunt gets here because Aunt Alma is too tender-hearted and not as practical as Big Luce, who might know what Pudge can do about his girl's chest. If Aunt Alma hears about it, she'll get mad at his mama, who is Aunt Alma's little sister. She'll say, "Why can't you buy that boy some clothes that fit?" There'll be a fight, and his mama will cry or his Aunt Alma will.

Pudge follows Big Luce through the back door of the Laundromat into the kitchen.

She pulls a couple of lemon ices from the refrigerator, hands Pudge one with a flat, wooden spoon.

Pudge would rather have any flavor but lemon. Lemon grabs at the back of your cheeks, right underneath your ears, and it just pulls at you. Every bite the same. Cool and nice and then pulling at you. It makes the fizzing feeling worse.

They go back outside to the round table in the courtyard, which is full of yellow hibiscus flowers. Big Luce brushes a few of the bright petals off the table. Puts one behind her ear, twirls another in front of Pudge. He likes to tip his face up and feel the flower brush on his closed eyes, but he shakes his head no because it's a nice thing, and nice things make him cry.

If you cry, his mama has told him, it only makes the bullies want to hurt you more. That doesn't make any sense to Pudge, but he knows it's true. When his baby sister cries, it only makes his father hit her more. Sometimes Pudge sneaks in after and holds Belinda's tiny baby hand. Belinda's a quick learner for a baby. Once she's been hit, she doesn't cry anymore. She just lies there in the footlocker that their father cleared out for a bed, looks at the ceiling while Pudge holds her hand. Pudge wishes he could tell Aunt Alma or Big Luce about the hitting, but it's a secret. His mother has warned him. "A family's business stays in the family," she told him. "I don't need an earful from your Aunt Alma or that other one. They don't know the first thing about families."

Big Luce sits next to Pudge in one of the old iron chairs. Pudge hates the narrow chairs, how they dig into his sides, but he can't just stand there like an idiot.

"So what's the scene, jelly bean?" Big Luce asks.

Pudge messes with his lemon ice, stalling. "I got into honors chorus," he says. Honors chorus is good news. Sort of. Focus on the positive, that's what Big Luce always tells him to do.

"I thought you weren't going to audition."

"I wasn't," Pudge says, "but then I did." He'll need a suit to be in honors chorus and how is he going to get one? Where do suits come from, anyway? *Titties,* he thinks again and then lets all the worried thoughts run together for a minute. He takes a bite of lemon ice and imagines that the pulling beneath his ears is pulling the bad thoughts out of his head, mixing them with ice so they can disappear down his throat. "I don't think I'm going to do it, though," he tells Big Luce. "There's a spring concert and you have to get permission and you wear a suit and it's a lot of practice and I might not want to go every day." Pudge knows better than to tell his mama that he needs a suit. It's the kind of thing she would forget to do, or if she remembered, she'd buy one for a regular-sized boy. For incentive.

"You should do it," Big Luce says. "You're the best singer I know."

It's tricky when someone says something nice. Pudge stares at the cement, takes a big bite of lemon ice and lets it pull hard at his cheeks. Tries not to let the nice thing make him cry. Like a titty baby. "You must not know many singers," Pudge says and waits.

Big Luce raises an eyebrow at him, which is about as mean as she ever gets. Even when he's being a smart aleck. Even when he's asking for it. She has her long legs crossed, and she swings one slowly, la-le-la, like there's nothing in the world to worry about.

"I don't know," Pudge says. "I haven't really decided. It might be boring."

Big Luce pulls her long braid over her shoulder and takes it loose from its rubber band. Pudge watches her hair spring free. "You don't know," he says. "It's a lot of work."

Big Luce's swinging leg goes la-le-la.

"Where do you go to get suits?" Pudge finally has to ask because he's not ready to say the titties part, and his ignorance, this particular ignorance, fills him with shame, and his throat stops the lemon ice from going down so that it burns instead of cooling and then it's pulling at his cheeks.

"Pudge, honey." Big Luce leans over and puts her hand on the knee of the stupid, tight pants, and then Pudge is crying because his eyes will cry even when he tells them not to.

Don't, he keeps saying to himself, biting down on his own teeth. Don't. But he cries because he's a titty baby. "I've got titties," he says. There's no more time. Aunt Alma will be walking through the gate any minute.

"What?" Big Luce asks.

Pudge sits up straight and pokes them out. "Titties," he repeats.

"Well, everybody's got titties, Pudge. The problem here is that you got a too-tight shirt."

This much Pudge knows. The question is how to make the titties go away. How to get a shirt that will hide them at least, a suit that's made for a boy Pudge's size. When Pudge suggested to his mother that maybe he should try on the clothes at the store to be sure of the fit, she just made that sound she makes when Pudge says something stupid, the *pshh*-ing sound. "I'm not hauling your fat ass from store to store so everyone can stare at me," she said. That's when his mother told him the thing about how small clothes would be an incentive to lose weight. "You got your pants cutting into that table muscle all day," she said, poking him in his belly, "you might think more about what you're shoving in your pie hole."

Big Luce squeezes Pudge's knee. "You got a man's chest and a boy's legs and arms." She puts her arm next to Pudge's. It's a lot longer. "See?" she says. "You're still growing. Pretty soon, your legs and arms will grow, and it'll all even out."

It could be true. It might be that he has a man's chest, Pudge thinks.

"Look at me," Big Luce says, standing up to toss their empty cups into the trash. "I used to be teensy till I grew."

Big Luce is six feet even. "You were short?" Pudge asks.

"I surely was. One year I needed a little step stool to hang up my clothes, the next year I didn't." Big Luce sits back down next to Pudge, pats his knee again. "Same thing will happen for you."

Pudge makes a muscle, even though it's a little kid thing to do. "Look at this." A muscle is proof that something good is on the way. Maybe when his arms grow out, he'll look like that guy, like Arnold Swarzanecken.

Big Luce gives the muscle a squeeze. "Not bad, Galahad," she says, like it's the best muscle in the world. Big Luce just loves everything. Aunt Alma, too. His mama and Aunt Alma are opposites. Pudge wonders if he and his sister will be opposites when they're grown.

A buzzer sounds from inside the laundry, and Big Luce goes in the open back door to pull clothes from the big industrial dryer. On her way in, she puts a hand under Pudge's chin and makes him look at her. "Aunt Alma and I are having a cookout tonight," she says. "I wish you'd come over for dinner."

There's nothing Pudge loves more than sitting with Big Luce and Aunt Alma and playing I Spy on the bayou outside their trailer. Even though he's too old for it. Even though his mother has told him not to hang out down there because Big Luce and Aunt Alma are an abomination, going against God's plan. The devil, she's said, will work through them to get at Pudge, so he should steer clear.

Once, Pudge made a mistake and bragged to his father that he and Big Luce had caught twenty-seven fish. He didn't say the part about how the fish were really hand bones—carpal, metacarpal, phalanges—or that fishing is what they call the game they play to help Aunt Alma study for her nurse's tests. His father didn't call Pudge a liar. Instead, the next weekend they had to go fishing so

Pudge could enlighten his father about his technique. That's the word his father used. *Enlighten* me. And then Pudge had to do the whole thing. The complicated fishing pole, the worm, the hook, pulling the scared fish from the water. And then it had to be hit with the club Pudge's father made from the end of a baseball bat. You had to hit it to make it stop flopping around, to put it out of its misery, his father said, like smashing it with the club was some sort of kindness. "Don't be such a titty baby," his father told Pudge when Pudge looked away from the fish while he smashed its skull with the bat. It was all Pudge's fault for exaggerating, for making his father think that he'd really gone fishing with Big Luce. It wasn't ever a good idea to mention her name at home, but sometimes Pudge just forgot.

Pudge's father is gone now, maybe for good this time, his mother says. At night, after the drinking starts and she's finished being mean, Pudge's mother sits on the sofa with Belinda, crying. It's better if Pudge comes home late when his mother is asleep on the couch with Belinda tucked in the crook of one arm. His sister knows to wait, to be quiet, and she just stares at whatever's in front of her until Pudge comes home and puts her to bed.

By the time Big Luce finishes pulling the clothes from the dryer and comes back outside, the sun has moved past the corner of the Laundromat, and it's firing into the courtyard. She opens the umbrella over the table, something Pudge could've done, if he'd only thought of it. Big Luce reaches over and pretends to steal his nose, which he has always loved. "We can make banana pudding tonight," she says.

Then right before Pudge expects it, Aunt Alma comes through the gate, still in her nurse's uniform, looking like an angel, clean and smart and happy to see him.

"Pudge!" she says and gives him that smile, all her teeth shining. "You coming to the cookout?"

Later that night, after the hot dogs and banana pudding, after Aunt Alma shows Pudge how to make a hat out of fishing line and a paper sack, Pudge starts home. When he gets to Palmyra Street, he decides to check on the closed Laundromat. Really, he wants to make a wish. The snack machine in the front of the Laundromat puts a light out on the sidewalk in front. If you make a wish while you walk through that light, the wish will come true. Pudge has proof. The night before tryouts for honors chorus at school, he wished to get picked. Pudge knows it was his walk through the snack machine light that got him a place with the altos.

For twenty-three days, Pudge has not walked through the snack machine light and wished for his father's return. It's what his mother cries for every night, but Pudge just can't bring himself to wish for what his mother wants. "People don't necessarily want what's good for them," he heard his Aunt Alma say to Big Luce in the kitchen this evening when they thought Pudge couldn't hear. "If she takes him back, I'm not going to stay out of it anymore." The refrigerator door slammed shut. "I'll kidnap her if I have to."

Tonight, when Pudge walks through the light, he wishes for things to even out, like Big Luce said. He wishes for his legs and arms to go ahead and grow. He wishes for his titties to turn to muscle.

When he gets home, the apartment is dark and quiet, but that isn't the part that worries Pudge. What worries Pudge is that his mother isn't asleep on the couch. What worries Pudge is the way Aunt Alma said, "If she takes him back again . . ." In Pudge's bedroom, the lid of the footlocker is closed with the front hasp flipped up to keep it from sealing shut. When he opens it, Belinda is sound asleep inside. Her little fingers curl and uncurl when Pudge touches them.

The door to his mother's bedroom is closed, and this can only mean one thing: Aunt Alma's going to have to kidnap his mother.

There's breakfast in the morning, everyone together, which is how it always is the first morning after his father comes back. Pudge's mother has somehow gotten a dozen eggs and a whole pound of bacon. Grits and biscuits. And there's butter that no one's watching Pudge take. His father is missing the little group of teeth that snap into the front of his mouth. After he's been gone awhile, Pudge's father almost never comes home with his teeth. The blank place makes him look like he's putting on an act meant to make people laugh.

"I was thinking I'd go around to American Can today," his father tells his mother. "See if maybe I can get on in sales."

"Oh, you'd be great at sales," Pudge's mother says in a cheerful voice, and he wonders how she knows this.

Belinda's in her high chair, grits all over her. She doesn't like to have food on her, and Pudge tenses up when she starts to moan. He puts a piece of bacon in his mouth and concentrates on the salty good taste. Belinda just wants someone to wipe her face. When Pudge stands up to do it, their father cuts him the eyes—tending babies is woman's work—so Pudge grabs another piece of toast instead and sits down. He crunches on the near-burnt bread to drown out whatever's coming. But his father surprises him and says a first-day-back kind of thing. "Hey baby," he says to Belinda, smiling. "Hey." He reaches for a clean spot on her arm and wags it. "Say, 'Hi, Daddy!' Say, 'Hi!'" Belinda stops moaning, goes completely still. Pudge imagines that eventually she'll be able to talk, to say what's bothering her. So far she hasn't said one word.

·

After school, Pudge walks to the grocery and hangs out reading *Muscle World* in the magazine aisle. Make a plan, Big Luce always says. Wishing is the first part of a plan. She was right about how Pudge's titties mean he has a man's chest; all the men in *Muscle World* have them. But their titties match the other bulges on their giant arms and legs.

Later, he goes to the Laundromat. Big Luce is out front talking to Deysi Hernandez's grandmother, who doesn't speak much English. Whenever she comes to the Laundromat, though, just like magic, Big Luce starts talking Spanish, too. Pudge can't imagine how she learned to do that. Maybe she wished for it, and it came to her.

Deysi Hernandez is the smallest girl in Pudge's class and the prettiest, Pudge thinks. Maybe the smartest, too. When she and her grandmother go shopping, Deysi does all the talking. Pudge gave her a secret valentine last year. She never said anything about it, so he guesses she hasn't figured out it was from him. If she's at the Laundromat today, he's going to ask her if she got an invitation to Jerry Beatty's party. Supposedly, everyone got one. It might be a trick on Pudge, or maybe not. Jerry Beatty's father is a minister, and his mother makes Jerry invite his whole class to things.

"There's folding in the back," Big Luce says, "if you'd like to make some money."

Folding means folding clean laundry. That's part of Big Luce's Laundromat business. Doing other people's laundry and bringing it to them all folded up. Pudge goes to the back and pulls warm towels and tablecloths from a big basket. After he folds everything, he wraps it up in brown paper and ties it with a string. He loves the brown paper. It's what he made Deysi's secret valentine with. He had hoped the paper would be a hint about who was "Crazy for Deysi!" Probably everyone is, though.

Pudge puts the brown packages in the insulated wooden box of Big Luce's delivery cart, which used to be her father's ice cream cart. Her father made the whole thing himself, the three-wheeled bike and the insulated box. All it took was some good old-fashioned ingenuity, Big Luce said.

Pudge wants to surprise Big Luce by getting the rack for the hanging clothes that goes on the bike. It's tall and wide, made from galvanized pipe, shaped like the chin-up bars at school. Pudge's arms aren't really long enough to carry it yet, but maybe there's another way to move it? Maybe drag it? In the courtyard's shed, he finds the rack leaning against the wall. He grabs one leg of the giant galvanized U and pulls on it, and then it's like the rack is alive. Yanking on one side throws the thing out of balance, and it swings around the shed with a mind of its own.

The rack knocks a shelf loose, and a pile of rusty, cast-iron window weights scatters, banging against the cement slab and rolling around so that Pudge almost slips on them. "Fuck!" Pudge says, then "Sorry, sorry," though no one can hear him out here. He puts the shelf back up and lays the weights on it just like Big Luce had them: eight pounders, then ten pounders, then twelve. A while back Big Luce said she planned to spray-paint them and use them for decoration.

Pudge does his best to get the shed straightened up, then goes out to sit in the courtyard until Big Luce comes for the rack. When she does, he watches her spread her arms and lift it easily.

"Big Luce," Pudge says, following her inside, "could I use a couple of those barbells from the shed?"

"Barbells?"

"You know, those weights. The ones from the back windows?"

"Oh sure. You can have all of them." Big Luce lifts the rack and fits it into the tubes on either side of the delivery cart. She checks the tags on the hanging clothes and puts them on the rack. "There's spray paint back there, too, if you want it. Red, I think."

Pudge doesn't want to get too excited in case the window weights are not the answer, but he does his Tarzan yell anyway. The window weights are as big around as the thick plantains in the grocery, only heavier, because they're made of iron.

After Aunt Alma gets to the Laundromat and Big Luce leaves with the deliveries, he sprays the rusty cylinders red. It makes them look official. He threads clothesline through the hanging loops of the weights, making twenty-pound loads that he carries around the block to his house, one load at a time. He has to rest a lot. In *Muscle World* it said you have to start small and work your way up. You have to do it every day or you won't get any results.

When he goes up the stairwell with the last load, he finds Aunt Alma in the kitchen talking with his mama. Aunt Alma has a quiet, asking voice, and his mama answers her with the pretend calm voice she uses to explain Pudge's father to other people.

"You and the kids can stay in our big trailer," Aunt Alma says. "Luce and I can hang out in the Airstream until you find a place that Clayton won't drag his ass back to."

"Nobody needs to go anywhere, Alma. Clayton is a man's man, and sometimes he needs to go off and do what men do. I don't expect you would understand that."

Pudge walks right past his mama and Aunt Alma to his bedroom without either of them saying a thing. He cuts the clothesline that's holding the weights together and lines them up under his bed, eights, then tens, then twelves. The twelves are as long as the bones from his foot to his knee (tibia and fibula), and he can't lift even one over his head. When he grabs one with both hands and yanks it into the air, he loses his balance and falls backward into the closet door, knocking the door off its track.

"What are you doing in there?" his mama yells.

"I'm fixing something," Pudge yells back. He goes to the hall closet and gets the little toolbox his father gave him for Christmas last year. He imagines having a three-wheel bike like Big Luce's, except the little chest would be filled with tools, and he could ride around and ask people if they had anything that needed fixing. After he gets the closet door back up, he turns to Belinda's bed. It shouldn't have a lid. It shouldn't. He unscrews the hinges and pulls the lid off and props it behind the footlocker. He might draw Belinda some pictures and tape them on the lid for her to look at. He hides the screws. He'll tell his father the lid came loose and fell off.

"I'm trying to save my marriage," he hears his mother say out in the living room. "You don't know what marriage is like. It takes work."

"Work. *Really?*"

"Who's going to support these kids, Alma?" Pudge hears the calm leak out of his mother's voice. "And a boy needs his father."

Pudge wants to tell his mother that he'd be okay if his father lived somewhere else. Somewhere Pudge could visit and leave. And take Belinda with him. Poor Belinda. She's got to stay wherever she's put because she's a baby. She can't deny doing wrong, can't turn their father's attention to something else when his anger starts to aim itself at her. She's stuck. They're all stuck, but somehow his mother can't see it.

In the mirror at the back of the Laundromat, Pudge barely recognizes himself. He buttons the suit coat that Aunt Alma and Big Luce bought him at J.C. Penney's when he told them that he was for sure going to stay in honors chorus. It's a great suit. No pinching or poking. His father said for Pudge to tell Aunt Alma that she can keep the fucking monkey suit, that last time he checked, he was still the head of his household, and he didn't need a couple of bull daggers dressing his son like a fruit. *Bull dagger* isn't in the dictionary. Pudge looked. Aunt Alma said he can keep the suit at the Laundromat and wear it anytime he wants. Clothes make the man, the lady at Penney's said. Pudge is going to wear the suit to Jerry Beatty's party today to see what kind of man it makes him.

When he gets to the Beattys' house, which is right next to Mid-City Methodist Church, a bunch of kids are standing around the dining room table waiting for someone to serve them punch. Deysi Hernandez is right near the front of the line. No adults in sight. Pudge is the only one in a suit, and it makes him feel grown up. He just walks right over to the punch bowl and lifts the silver ladle like he knows what he's doing.

"Ladies first," Pudge says and hands a cup of punch to Deysi with a nod.

"Thank you," Deysi says, and she looks at Pudge like he's something special.

When he finishes serving punch to the other kids, Pudge walks out to the backyard where several mothers are cooking hot dogs and hamburgers and running back and forth setting everything up.

Pudge hopes he can get through the party without messing up his new suit. He should probably take off the jacket at least. Without it, though, he goes back to being round at the bottom and round at the top, the strip of belt like an equator separating his halves.

Jerry Beatty and some of the other boys from Pudge's class are standing around the table in their regular clothes. A stack of plates sits next to a pile of matching napkins, and little weights hang on the tablecloth to keep it from flying up. It's a very fancy party, and Pudge feels proud to be wearing a suit.

"Hey, Pudge!" Jerry calls out and waves Pudge over. Pudge adjusts his tie like he's seen men do. "Excuse me," he says to Deysi, who's walked out behind him and isn't really talking to him exactly. He says it in case she was fixing to.

"What's with the suit?" Jerry asks. "Somebody die?"

Pudge wonders if this is about his mother and his father and their fighting. Sometimes the police come. Once, an ambulance. He keeps his mouth shut, raises an eyebrow like Big Luce does when somebody's being a smartass.

"Dearly beloved," one of the other tough boys starts and then all the boys are laughing. Pudge laughs, too, in case the joke isn't about him.

"Hey, Spud," Jerry says to the slow boy from their class, the one with the big, wide eyes and the flat face. "Have another hot dog, why don't you."

The boy keeps his eyes on the table, tells Jerry he's full. One of the tough boys loads up a hot dog and holds it in front of Spud's face. "Come on, Spud," Jerry says. "However many hot dogs you can eat, I bet I can eat one more."

The kid looks terrified. Any minute now he'll pee his pants, which is the result Jerry's after.

"You too scared to bet somebody you can't beat?" Pudge asks. It's like a whole different boy is working Pudge's mouth. Or maybe it's the man that the suit has made Pudge into.

"Shut up, Fudge," one of the tough boys says. "Jerry's not talking to you."

"Cuz he's scared, I guess," Pudge's suit makes him say. Like it's a suit of armor and not a hundred percent polyester.

"Ohhh," the boys all say. "Look out!"

Pudge's hand crosses the table to take the hot dog.

"Okay," Jerry says. "Okay. You first."

Pudge finishes the first hot dog easily. Spud moves away from the table but watches from across the yard. Pudge begins to clear the plate of hot dogs that Mrs. Beatty has just set out next to a basket of toasted buns.

He watches his hands swim like a couple of fish back and forth between the plate and his mouth. The fish are so quick that Pudge has to swallow without chewing to keep up with them. He checks to see if Deysi is watching this moment, the best moment of his entire year. She's not. Several girls are admiring Deysi's new earrings, giant silver loops her mother sent for her birthday. No one knows where Deysi's mother is, only that she sends things now and then.

The tough boys begin to laugh. They punch each other on the arm. Jerry Beatty might win at sports, might always be the teacher's favorite, but today he will have to admit that nobody can beat Pudge Morris in an eating contest. Pudge's mouth is still working on hot dogs nine and ten when Jerry's mother comes out with a jar of relish. "Who ate all the hot dogs?" she asks, searching the boys' faces. "Now there won't be enough for everybody."

"Piggy-piggy-Pu-udge, Piggy-piggy-Pu-udge," all the boys chant.

Mrs. Beatty looks right at Pudge, and Pudge twists away, his mouth overflowing with evidence. When he turns, his eyes meet Deysi's.

Without even swallowing, Pudge takes off running for the Laundromat, where he hopes Big Luce will have extra clothes for him. He doesn't want to look at the unlucky suit for another second.

On Monday, several of Pudge's classmates make snorting pig sounds in the lunch line. "Save some for the rest of us!" Jerry Beatty yells from the back and everyone laughs. Even Spud, whose pig snorts seem the loudest. No one's allowed to leave the lunch line, but as soon as Pudge gets his plate of food, he walks directly to the garbage and dumps it. In the bathroom, he closes himself in one of the stalls. He makes a fist and pounds it against the cinder-block wall in 3/4 time. "Carpal-metacarpal-phalanges-*and*-trapezium-trapezoid-capitate-*and*," he says, smashing each of the twenty-seven fishbones of the hand that grabbed all those hot dogs, the hand that has made so much trouble for him.

Pudge's father likes everyone to sit down to dinner together. The only problem is that there's no telling when his father will be home. He hasn't gotten a job yet, and now Pudge's mother has started to complain again. On top of that, Belinda cries all the time because she's cutting teeth. Aunt Alma said it really hurts.

It's nine o'clock. Pudge's mother and Belinda are lying on the couch asleep. Pudge is lifting weights. After Jerry's party, he decided to step up his routine to twice a day, before breakfast and before dinner. He hasn't eaten since breakfast, and he's hungry.

He can hold both eight-pounders over his head, can raise and lower them, one and two and three and four. He still can't get the twelve-pounder in the air with just one hand. Once, when he was mad, he got it over his head. When he tried to jerk it up a second time, he lost his balance again but caught himself before he fell into the closet door. He's getting there. Last night he made a twelve-pound wish and walked through the light of the snack machine at the Laundromat.

He's tired, and he's lost count of the lifts he's made. The good smell of dinner and his missing father are starting to get on his nerves. He goes into the kitchen for a drink of water and takes a peek at the macaroni and cheese warming in the oven. He wants to open the door and snap off the wave of burnt cheese that's curling over the edge of the casserole dish, but his father will know it was him. Pudge's right hand is sore from this afternoon's pounding, so it's his left hand he smacks with the meat tenderizer that he pulls from the kitchen drawer. Carpal-metacarpal-phalanges-*and.* The battered fish of his hands are hungrier than ever. They swim, confused and determined to the handle on the oven door, which suddenly stands open so that Pudge can sniff at his dinner. The fish swim around the back of the casserole, bite off a crust of cheese and swim back to Pudge with their trouble. And then they move on to the pantry, where the only food that his father won't notice missing is a small can of Crisco. The fish dive in and jump out, each time carrying a gob of slick food to Pudge's face. Eat. Eat. Eat. Until the hungry mouth of the distal phalange is sucking along the bottom seam of the can. And Pudge is full. And queasy.

Pudge's father rolls in at about ten-thirty, and he's happy and talkative like he is sometimes. Luckily, Pudge's mother wakes right up, tucks Belinda into her high chair and goes to the oven for their dinner without complaining.

"I was talking to Hernandez," his father says to the room. "Not the one who shot What's Her Face's-father-the-ice-cream-man, the other one. What's his name?"

"Arturo," his mother says. "The other one's still in prison, I think."

"Well, Arturo is talking about setting up a little seafood shop, using it as a front to run numbers. You know what that means?" Pudge's father grabs his mother and pulls her onto his lap, smooches on her neck. "Do you know what that means, little girl?"

"Arturo's wife is gonna have a house full of fish stink?"

"No, wiseass. It means we're gonna be rich because Arturo needs a supplier for the fish part of the operation. I fish. And this one right here," Pudge's father says, pointing at Pudge, who's sitting down waiting for the macaroni, his head throbbing, his stomach heavy, "this one can really fish. Right? Twenty-seven in one day, he and What's-Her-Face caught."

Pudge nods. He sees his future: stabbing worms with hooks, pulling fish from their families, hitting them in the head. Saying sorry, sorry, sorry to his father all the livelong day.

In her high chair, Belinda moans a little.

"You want to help your old man make a mint?"

"Yessir," Pudge says, though he doubts he's said it right. Saying things too loud or not loud enough always means trouble. He makes a wish right then that Aunt Alma will kidnap his family before any of this happens.

"Well, don't be such a baby about it," his father commands. "Say it like you mean it."

"Yessir, I'll help," Pudge says again. Maybe the right way, maybe not.

"Well, I sure don't want to put you out or anything. I mean, I'd hate to keep you away from the feed trough and your singing career." His father runs his hands up his mother's dress, and his mother squirms and slaps at him. Maybe a play slap. Maybe a real one. It's hard to know at first. "A big star like yourself," his father says, "won't need to learn to do an honest day's work, I don't guess."

"Sorry," Pudge says. Belinda starts to cry just then, and Pudge tries to talk over the crying. "I could help after chorus. And on the weekends. That's when the fish are best anyway." Pudge doesn't look at Belinda. His father doesn't take his eyes off of her.

Pudge's mother pulls at his father's shirt. "She's teething," she says, and Pudge hopes she won't say the other, but she does. "And she's tired. If you'd come home for dinner at a reasonable hour, she could go to bed. We all could."

Pudge's father jumps up from the table and grabs Belinda by one arm and carries her like a rag doll to the bedroom. Pudge and his mother follow, but not too close. "Who took this fucking lid off?" he yells.

Pudge runs in behind his father. "It fell off," he says, dodging his father's backhand. His father pulls the lid from behind the footlocker and slams it down over the chest. Inside, Belinda cries her screeching scared cry.

"Look at this," Pudge says and pulls an eight-pounder out from under the bed. He does a couple of curls with it.

Pudge's father punches the lid of the footlocker with his fist, yells, "Shut up!" The fist goes up over his head and then wham! Shut up! In just a minute, he'll pull the lid off and use that hand on Belinda. Pudge is sure of it.

"I can lift the twelve-pounder, too," Pudge says, and his father looks up at last. Pudge bends and pulls the twelve-pounder out and, with one hand, swings it up into the air as fast as he can to show that twelve pounds is nothing, that Pudge knows the meaning of hard work.

Belinda goes on screaming. It's like she's trying to get their father to hit her.

Pudge watches all twenty-seven fish of his father's closed hand bounce off the lid of the footlocker. Carpal, metacarpal, phalanges, they jump and dive until they finally break through. When they surface again, there's bleeding. Shut up! Shut up! All together those fish dive into the footlocker—over and over they dive—until, out of kindness, Pudge aims the twelve-pounder at their suffering and swings.

Killer Heart

Dooley and Tina are fighting. Or not fighting, Dooley guesses, but discussing. That's what Tina calls it, anyway. They have most of their discussions while their three-year-old daughter, Gracie, is at her grandmother's across the lake. Today Dooley decides that if he shows a positive attitude and keeps his comments to a minimum, they might be able to wrap things up in the next little bit. There's a show about the Louisiana black bear coming on in half an hour, and Dooley hopes he won't have to miss it.

"It's just that you're so impulsive, Dooley," Tina says, shifting to the general list of his faults. She's pacing back and forth, back and forth, like a little engine that's powered by fussing.

Tina keeps a record of old mistakes handy on a constant loop, one finger always hovering over the *play* button. During any dispute, when she's through with what is currently troubling her, she presses that button and everything stored on the loop begins to replay. In their house, the past is never over. The good news, though, is that once Tina gets to the Great Loop of Faults, it usually means the discussion is coming to an end.

"You never think things through," Tina goes on. "There's never a plan for anything."

"Maybe so," Dooley says in his upbeat, fight-ending tone, "but everything in the world can't be planned out, Tina. Gracie wasn't planned," he says, "and aren't you glad we have her?"

Instead of ending the discussion, this seems to wind Tina up even more. She starts back in with his faults, reciting one after another as though she's building a case. Dooley leans back in his big blue recliner and goes on clipping his toenails. He wonders if maybe he can get one of those prefab storage sheds for the backyard. He needs a place he can go to be alone and play his guitar as loud as he wants. If he soundproofs it, he can use the little shed as a recording studio.

Dooley misses his music, and he hasn't been able to make Tina understand that driving a forklift all day, picking up crates and moving them from one place to another, makes him feel trapped and lonely. He didn't move to New Orleans to drive a fucking forklift. A couple of months ago, for his twenty-second birthday, Dooley sat in with his old band. He told Tina that he wanted to start playing with them again, and the selfishness of this wish is one of the many items stored on the playback loop.

Tina heaves a sigh, and Dooley imagines that she's finally going to put the brakes on. That's when he'll get up from his recliner and go to her. He'll pull her close, hug her head to his chest so she can hear that his heart is still full of love for her. "Baby," he'll say. "I'm not built for arguing. You know that. I'm built for love." And he'll say he's sorry if he made her sad or mad or frustrated, depending on which she is. That part always requires a little guesswork.

Or maybe today Dooley won't be at fault. Sometimes, fussing is just Tina's way of working something out in her head, and when Dooley apologizes, Tina will say, "No, baby, that was just me blowing steam." Every now and then, Dooley knows, staying home with Gracie makes Tina feel like she's missing out on things. He isn't the only one who's made sacrifices for their daughter.

As Dooley is getting up to go to his pacing wife, though, she says something that knocks him back into his recliner.

"Gracie's not yours," she says.

Dooley searches Tina's face to see what she's up to. "Not mine, how?"

"Not yours as in Toby Tidwell is her biological father."

"Fuck you, Tina. That's not funny." Dooley eases forward and perches on the edge of his chair. He feels a toenail clipping under his hand, sharp and painful, but he doesn't move. Not even a little.

Tina goes to the desk in the kitchen and pulls some papers out of a drawer that Dooley could've opened any time he wanted, though he never has. Why not? Tina is crying now, and she puts the papers in Dooley's hand saying, "Sorry, baby, I'm so sorry."

Tina's mother paid for Tina and Dooley to go see a genetic counselor where they and Gracie were all given DNA tests. Tina read on the Internet that a DNA test would show if Gracie had inherited the going-deaf gene from Tina's family or if she'd gotten Dooley's genes on that score.

Looking at the results, Dooley can't be happy or relieved that Gracie has been spared a future of progressive hearing loss. The report says there's a 99.9 percent chance that Toby Tidwell—when did he get tested?—is Gracie's father. Dooley wants to go get fucking Toby Tidwell and string him up by the ankles. Bleed him like the pig he is. Toby Tidwell got busted up in a tank accident while practicing whatever people in the Army practice, so Dooley will have to wait till he gets out of Walter Reed to bust Toby up himself.

"Tina," Dooley moans, shoving the papers between the arm and seat cushion of his recliner. He wants to ask if she's in love with Toby Tidwell now or if this is all in the past. Does the past cancel out Tina's love for Dooley? Dooley's love for Gracie? Dooley can't tell. Nor can he tell what the numbers and letters on the DNA test mean for him and his little family. The swimming equation is just too hard to follow. He needs some air.

Jumping up from the recliner, Dooley jerks open the back door, flies down the steps and scrambles across the lawn. He shoots past the place he'd been thinking of putting his music studio and doesn't stop until he reaches the back fence that separates his long, narrow yard from his neighbor's. Up close like that, Dooley can see through the gaps between the fence boards into his neighbor's yard where a pool shimmers in the late afternoon light. It looks peaceful over there, a little slice of heaven, where no one ever argues, where no one keeps secrets or lies. Dooley has never heard a single sound from that house, never heard splashing or conversation on the deck. Maybe no one even lives there. One thing is for sure, though: You can't tell what's going on just by looking. Earlier this afternoon, Dooley had been a man with a wife and a child, and he bet he still looked like one, too.

Dooley and Tina agree that they should take a break. Dooley will get an apartment, and Gracie will stay in the house with Tina. They'll see what happens after that. Dooley doesn't want to move out. He doesn't want his daughter to stop being his daughter, but he isn't sure he wants Tina to go on being his wife. At first he'd thought, *It's just a piece of paper with numbers. It doesn't change a thing.* But every time he asks Tina if she's going to tell Toby Tidwell that Gracie is his baby, she sends a question right back: You'd want to know, wouldn't you? That paper, those numbers, he realizes, are going to change everything.

Tina says they have to prepare Gracie for when Dooley moves out. She says maybe they should sit down as a family and talk to her, but Dooley says no. He'll tell her himself.

"You've done enough, thank you very much," he says to Tina.

"Well, why don't you just put a scarlet *A* on me, and we can call it a day," Tina fires back.

She's hurt, and Dooley's glad of it. He decides to take Gracie to the mall. She needs shoes, and Dooley guesses he can tell her the moving-out stuff over lunch at the food court.

"Are you going to let Gracie call Toby 'Daddy'?" he asks Tina when he tells her his food court plan. But everything is *I don't know, Dooley, I don't know* with Tina. He wants her to say of course not, that Gracie will only ever have one daddy, and that is Dooley. Always and forever have disappeared from the scene, though, and it looks like divorce is coming in to take their place.

"We were having problems before the DNA test," Tina tells Dooley, as though the test is what made Gracie not his. "You knew that." But, of course, he hadn't known, and he wondered how anyone ever knew anything, how Tina knew, for instance, which were the end-of-the-line problems and which were the par-for-the-course problems.

"I need your keys," he says when he's ready to go to the mall.

"Put the car seat in your truck, Dooley. I need to go across the lake and see Mama."

Tina's a pretty competent woman, but driving a stick is not among her many talents, and Dooley's truck is a standard. There's only the one car seat, and Dooley is a little afraid of it. Tina usually puts Gracie in it and takes her out, and he's already nervous about having to do that without the added hassle of having to uninstall the stupid seat and put it in his truck.

"I thought we weren't supposed to put the car seat in a truck."

"That's just if you have airbags," Tina points out. "You don't have airbags."

"Maybe I should get a car seat for my truck, then, so we don't have to switch back and forth after I move."

"What for?" Tina says, and Dooley begins to grasp the size of the changes ahead.

He goes out and unhitches the car seat from Tina's car. He bought the little Chevy for Tina when Gracie was born. Cost him five hundred bucks, but he fixed it up and it rides fine now. Both vehicles are parked on the street, and the air inside them is hot and thick. By the time he gets the car seat installed in his little low-rider truck and Gracie strapped into it, they're both sweating so much that he thinks maybe they should just have their little conversation right there and be done with it. His AC is broken, but the fan still works, and he turns it on high. The sudden blast of hot air blows Gracie's damp black hair straight up. Her long lashes lower to protect her eyes, and a bright, even line of teeth light up her happy toddler smile. Dooley wonders how he could've thought he had anything to do with such perfection.

Tina comes out carrying her lunch pail of a purse, which Dooley calls the Bottomless Can of Infinite Mystery. Are the DNA papers in there? She leans in Dooley's window and tells him that he needs to get Gracie home by two, so she can get a nap. "I don't want her waking me up in the middle of the night because she fell asleep too early," Tina tells Dooley in a pissed-off kind of tone, like he's already failed to get Gracie home in time.

Dooley fiddles with the air vents.

"Dooley?"

"Two o'clock. Nap. I got it, Tina." Dooley turns the steering wheel toward the street and pulls off.

At the mall, he leaves the truck's fan running so it can blow on Gracie while he tries to disengage her from the car seat. The buckle had clicked shut easily enough, but getting it open is another thing altogether. Tina always makes it look easy. Because he's tall, Dooley has to stand outside the low truck, bend his knees and lean over nearly double to reach his daughter. His hands are big, and he fumbles with the clasps while Gracie wiggles and kicks the dashboard. It takes a few tries before he finally gets the contraption undone.

"Come on, Gracie," Dooley says, wiping his sweaty forehead on his sleeve. "Help Daddy help you." No, he decides, he will never in a million years let her call Toby Tidwell *Daddy*. "Airplane!" he says, holding his hands up in the air.

Gracie raises her arms and leans toward the door so Dooley can pull her out and fly her around the parking lot.

In the food court, there's a row of flashing, blinking machines along the back wall. Dooley holds Gracie up so she can play a game of Whack-A-Mole, which she's better at than Dooley would've guessed a three-year-old would be. After a few games, they go surfing for food. Gracie chooses pizza, which she loves but still can't pronounce. "Peace," is what it sounds like to Dooley when Gracie points at her food of choice.

"Right on," Dooley says, showing Gracie the peace sign.

In the middle of their meal, Dooley's phone rings. It's Tina.

"Did you get her shoes yet?"

"We're still eating."

"Goddammit, Dooley, it's one-thirty. Don't pull this on me today. Just skip the shoes. You're not going to be the one who has to get up with her in the middle of the night."

Tina hates that Dooley never hears Gracie calling from her room at night. He's a sound sleeper, *or pretends to be,* an accusation that is included in the call to his cell phone. Tina's exhausted, Dooley can tell. They both are. She says a few other things to him, and Dooley picks the olives off of his pizza while he waits for the talking to end. "Okay," he says when it does, and he hangs up. He watches Gracie pull wads of cheese off her pizza then gnaw at them with her itty-bitty teeth. She's too little for the moving-out speech. He'll have to find some other way to tell her what's what.

After lunch, Dooley takes Gracie to the self-serve shoe store where he lets her try on whatever interests her, including a pair of sparkling stiletto heels across the aisle from the children's section. She puts her hands on a chair, steps into the twinkling shoes, and Dooley walks her around the displays before going on to more sensible selections. Finally, she chooses a pair of miniature pink high tops. Dooley and Tina have been teaching Gracie how to use Velcro, and she's excited to be able to fasten her new shoes.

"Pink!" she says as they walk across the mall's vast parking lot.

"PinkPinkPink," Dooley says in time to Gracie's quick little steps.

Dooley opens the passenger door and lets some of the heat out before he feeds Gracie into the foot well. He pats the car seat. "Giddyup now."

Gracie squats in the foot well, messing with the Velcro on her shoes.

Dooley lifts his squirming daughter—Toby Tidwell's daughter? Impossible—into the car seat, which seems to have worked loose from the seat belt that is meant to hold it in place. Why has Tina put up with this piece of shit for so long? Dooley puts Gracie back in the foot well and struggles to rethread the seat belt. Sweat soaks his shirt while he fumbles with the clasps of the pain-in-the-ass seat.

Half a mile from home, on Magazine Street, Dooley notices a store called Wonderful Baby in a row of old shotgun houses that have been converted into upscale boutiques. How is it that he's never noticed it in all this time? In the shop's window, Dooley sees what is surely the Cadillac of car seats. He turns into the crumbling brick parking lot, which runs down the side of the boutique. He's not all that late. If he has his own car seat, he can take Gracie out more, and Tina can go visit her friends. Design for success, that's what Dooley's sister always tells him. No way is Toby Tidwell just going to waltz off with Dooley's baby girl. Fuck that noise. Dooley will have the car seat all ready, and his relationship with his daughter will go on just the way it is.

He turns to Gracie, who has been playing with the slide for his guitar, smacking it against the metal clasp of the car seat. She has fallen asleep with her fingers wrapped around it. Perfect, Dooley thinks. Tina can't yell at him about the missed nap after all. He kisses Gracie's sweaty forehead and tugs the metal slide out of her fist so she won't hurt herself. He rolls the windows up, leaving a couple of inches for air, then locks the doors so Gracie will be safe.

Inside Wonderful Baby, the salesladies all say that the car seat in the window is the best one on the planet. The best. And they offer to take Dooley's order because the one in the window, the last one in the store, is bolted to a two-by-four. Dooley says he wouldn't mind getting it loose if it means he can take it home today. And he'll pay full price, too. He'll show Tina that he isn't going to just step aside. He's Gracie's daddy. Nothing can change that.

When Dooley bounces down the front steps of the boutique, it's with the best car seat on the planet tucked under his arm. He rounds the corner of the building and starts into the little brick parking lot, where he sees a woman trying to break the driver's side window of his truck. Before he can call out to her, the window shatters and a second woman reaches in and opens the door. She pulls Gracie out of the car seat in what seems a single motion. *How?* Dooley wonders first, and then *why. Why?*

Within seconds of reaching his truck, a cop car and an ambulance scream into the parking lot, spewing uniformed men. The woman won't let Dooley touch Gracie, who is limp in her arms. His daughter has been sick on her brand-new shoes. Dooley tackles the woman holding his child, worried that she will get away before the cops can catch her. The cops pull Dooley off the woman and cuff him. The other woman, the one who broke his truck's window, hauls off and punches him in the chest. "Jackass!" she yells and then busts out crying.

Dooley screams bloody murder in the back of the hot cruiser, where they've hog-tied him. Gracie is taken away in the ambulance, and the cops want to know how to reach Dooley's wife. No one will answer when Dooley asks why. On the way to the police station, the cop who isn't driving looks over the back of his seat at Dooley. "You know how hot it was in that truck?"

"I wasn't gone but a few minutes," Dooley says, though he knows getting the car seat loose from its display had taken a while. "And I left the windows cracked so air could get in."

The cop shakes his head. "Windows open, windows closed. Doesn't make much difference in this heat. Especially in a black truck like that. Don't you watch the news?"

Dooley remembers a story about a baby dying from heatstroke in a car earlier that summer. The mother had left her infant in the backseat while she went gambling. But she'd been gone for hours. Dooley hadn't been gone long at all. "Gracie was sleeping," Dooley explains. "She has to have a nap, or she wakes my wife up at night."

"In this kind of heat, it doesn't take but ten, fifteen minutes," the cop goes on. He's pretty worked up. "A baby like that gets overheated, you know what happens?" the cop asks. "Her little heart explodes, that's what."

Dooley feels himself float up out of his body, up to the ceiling of the cruiser. He looks down on his pathetic form where it's hog-tied in the backseat. *It's just a body down there,* he thinks with his brain, which he can't get away from. *It's just a body.*

The next day, Tina bails Dooley out of jail with a credit card she borrowed from her mother. When Tina suggested that Dooley call his sister for the money, he begged her to leave Delia out of it. "I'll tell her myself, Tina," he says. "Just not yet." Dooley's sister is crazy about Gracie. And about Dooley, too, though he guesses that's all over now.

At the hospital where they go to sign for Gracie's body, a social worker suggests they get some grief counseling. When they get in the car to go home, Tina has a suggestion of her own. She suggests Dooley move out. Immediately. "You did this to get back at me!" Tina yells, leaning forward and jabbing her finger into Dooley's chest. "And now you're going to have to live with it!" There's something unhinged, something Dooley has never seen, in Tina's eyes.

When she finally gets to the end of the awful words, she begins to sob. She punches on Dooley's arm like a tiny boxer at the end of a too-long workout. Dooley half wants to give her his face to beat on, but he stays curled up in the corner of the passenger seat bawling.

It turns out Tina meant what she said about Dooley moving out. The day after Gracie's funeral, Dooley staggers up the steps just before dawn. He's put in a long, long day on a barstool where he attempted to get some relief from the bad pictures in his mind. When he puts his key in the lock, nothing happens. Well, one thing happens. The key gets stuck, and Dooley twists it until the metal shears, leaving the business end wedged in the keyhole. Tina, who is very handy, has apparently changed the lock.

Dooley falls to his knees, leans over and hollers his confusion through the mail slot and into his dark house. "Tell me what I should do," he yells, even though he knows Tina hates yelling.

"I'm not deaf yet," she always says. Because of the bad-hearing gene, most of the people in Tina's family, young and old, are somewhere on their way to being deaf, so family gatherings are loud. Outside those gatherings, Tina can't stand the sound of a raised voice.

Dooley sits down next to the door and smacks his head on the jamb until a lamp goes on inside, and he hears the *shick-shick-shick* of Tina trying to light the near-empty Bic that Dooley keeps on the key rack. He sits in the dark and the mosquitoes, facing the mail slot in the door. The door groans a little when Tina sits down and leans against it. Dooley smells a cigarette.

They've never smoked inside, and they both quit altogether when Tina got pregnant with Gracie. That's when she dropped out of college, too, and Dooley stopped playing with the band so he wouldn't have to travel on the weekends. He wonders, sitting on the doorstep, not why Tina is smoking inside, but why she's smoking at all. Isn't it important to go on taking good care of herself? Dooley wonders why everything has to change at once.

"Tell me what I should do," Dooley whispers through the mail slot.

"You've got to move on, Dooley."

Dooley asks her how. How can he move on? Tina always has opinions.

"You're the only one who knows for sure, Dooley," she whispers back, a stranger.

Every time Tina exhales, smoke curls at the brass lips of the mail slot like an answer, but then a back draft sucks most of it inside, where Dooley imagines it falls apart.

"Just tell me what you think," Dooley says, trying to get the old Tina, his bossy girl, to talk to him.

"What I think," she says, "doesn't have a thing to do with it anymore." Tina's smoky reply hangs there in the humid July air. She sounds broken, and Dooley wishes he knew something to say besides *sorry.* The week before, after she bailed him out of jail, she told him he was going straight to fucking hell. And then the thing about how Gracie's death was just Dooley's way of getting back at her. She apologized later. She said *sorry.* But it just about ruined Dooley for good the way something as big as what has happened to the two of them could end with the same word you'd say to a stranger you'd knocked into accidentally. He wasn't interested in ever hearing *sorry* again.

"You've got to find some other place to go," Tina says now. "You don't live here anymore."

Though her mouth is only inches away, Dooley can barely comprehend what she's saying. There's a buzzing in his ears, like his head is a jar of bees.

"Go to Delia's house, Dooley," Tina says. "She'll take care of you."

Dooley can't stay at his sister's. He can't stay anywhere. Everywhere he goes, there's always the look and then the whisper behind the hand, *Can you imagine?*

Dooley walks the half mile to his truck, which is still parked on the side of Wonderful Baby. He lets the tailgate down and crawls into the bed, where he stares at the big blank sky until the bees in his head buzz him to sleep.

Tina's car is gone when Dooley scales the fence that surrounds what used to be his backyard. He'll have to leave before Tina comes home because if she finds him there again, she said, she will personally shoot him. He wishes someone would shoot him, but not Tina. She doesn't know how her life would change in an instant if she did such a thing, even if a judge says it wasn't on purpose and gives her community service.

When he gets to the tall windows at the back of the house, he peers in. He's hoping to catch sight of some clues as to how it is that everything he understood to be true a few weeks ago could have vanished so quickly and with so little warning. He looks with longing at his old blue recliner and the Gibson acoustic that Tina gave him last Christmas. "He's got killer heart," she used to tell her friends about his guitar playing. "When he sings, it just breaks me into little pieces."

He's sweating so hard in the moist heat that he has to sit on the back steps to rest for a minute. The bees in his head have gotten worse. They get upset easily now, and Dooley spends his days trying to keep them quiet. At this particular moment the whole hive is pulsing with sound. Dooley shakes his head, but they keep at it. He turns and leans just a little so he can see into his old living room. In the corner nearest the window, stuck behind a potted rubber tree, he catches sight of a single sock, a tiny yellow one with ducks around the top. The bees object and start a steady drone in A-minor. Their dark chord of disapproval makes his heart go all speedy despite the twelve-pack of beer he drank this morning in hopes of keeping it still. When the bees get as loud as they are now, it sounds like a thousand people all saying, *ohhh*. Not the good *ohhh* of understanding, not the ecstatic *ohhh* of sex, but the tail end of the *N-ohhh!* of disbelief.

Suddenly, the buzzing is drowned out by the familiar squeal of the slipping power-steering belt on Tina's car. Dooley gets up too fast, and the beer and the heat pull his legs out from under him. He lands bony-ass first on a tree root. Once he gets upright, he skitters across the yard and hurls his lanky frame up onto the back fence, a maneuver that goes better than he expects. He lowers himself onto the deck that runs all the way around his neighbor's pool. The noonday sun blasts off the water in a hundred tiny lights that flash at Dooley like a mob of newspaper photographers. "Why'd you do it?" the reporters all want to know.

The monster Victorian faces Magazine Street and, along with its neighbors, blocks tourists' view of the run-down rental properties of the Irish Channel, among which is Dooley and Tina's little rented shotgun house. Dooley has often studied the elaborate landscaping through the gaps in the wooden fence. Up close, it's really, really nice.

He cuts down the Victorian's side yard and walks right out to the front of the house without anyone saying boo. He goes up the house's steps and rings the bell. *Jeffrey Mathers,* it says on the mailbox. Jeffrey is gone today, or maybe he's always been gone. Maybe it's only his name that's here.

Dooley goes back down the alley to the deck, to the pool. He can stay here, he thinks. Just hang out by the pool and keep an eye on his old house and his former wife. Maybe Jeffrey would prefer that Dooley not hang out in his pool, but it's not like Dooley's stealing anything. He just needs someplace clean and uncomplicated where he can make a plan. He'll have to move on. He knows that. He just doesn't know how yet. Or where.

Dooley sways on Jeffrey's deck, staring into the blue of the pool water, his heart pounding, the buzzing in his head a constant *ohhh.* He's got a little something for those bees, though. He kicks off his flip-flops at the pool's edge, turns his back to the water and lets himself fall in, jeans and all. The water looks soft, but it's not. The big blue hand of it slaps hard against Dooley's back, and for a minute the shock of the slap and the sting of chlorine override the buzzing, giving Dooley a little peace.

He loves the pool, how he can put his head under the water and watch the slow motion of his paddling arms. He wishes everything in life could be slowed down the way it is in the pool. It would be great if everyone could roll over and float when they got tired of paddling out there in the world. Dooley's always wanted a pool, and he sees now that having one is just as nice as he imagined. How many things turn out that way in life, just as nice as you think they're going to be?

When his legs feel too heavy to kick through the water, Dooley hooks his elbows over the side of the pool and stares through the

French doors into Jeffrey's empty kitchen. If he could just sit down inside there, away from the glare and the heat, maybe Dooley could gather his thoughts, which is hard to do with all the buzzing in his head. He listens to see what the bees think of the plan. *Go on ahead,* they buzz.

He hauls himself out of the pool and squishes over to the kitchen door. From his soaked pocket, he pulls his Swiss Army knife and goes right to work prying the retainer molding from one of the panes in Jeffrey's hundred-and-twenty-year-old back door. Suctioning the glass to the palm of his wet hand, he pulls it free and reaches in to turn the deadbolt. Once he's inside, Dooley puts the glass back in and the molding back on, something he hopes will show Jeffrey that he means no harm.

The second he steps into Jeffrey's kitchen, Dooley feels a plan hatch inside him. He'll be Jeffrey's roommate. He can watch over his house, maybe make him something tasty right here in this elaborate kitchen, which, from the looks of it, Jeffrey doesn't spend much time in. Dooley guesses that, theoretically, you'd want to get to know somebody before you asked him to move in with you, but his recent experience has illustrated for him that you can't ever really know someone. You can't even know yourself. If it turns out that Jeffrey doesn't want to get to know Dooley or have a roommate, then fine; Dooley will go back to sleeping in the bed of his truck.

The appliances in the kitchen are beautiful and perfect. So clean. Dooley wonders if anything bad could ever happen to someone with such a kitchen. There's an old-fashioned, stainless steel toaster on the counter. When he pushes its black handle all the way down, the toaster's interior brightens. Dooley can feel the heat of it, hear the hot, buzzing heart of it. He bends over and rests his chin on the counter and studies the face of the man on the shiny surface of the toaster. He makes a game of trying to look at both of the man's eyes at the same time. If he can do it, he decides, then his heart will stop, and it will all be over. At first, the man in the toaster looks confused and sad. When Dooley picks up the appliance to study the face more closely, the man looks surprised, and Dooley throws the hot thing into the sink. Pink cushions of blister inflate on the tips of his fingers, and he presses them into the cool fabric of his wet jeans.

He clumps over to the little bar and snatches a tumbler off a shelf. He means to fill it with water, but his hand chooses bourbon instead. Bourbon always makes him throw up, but first there'll be a struggle not to, and that's the best part of any day. He pours a tumbler full and sniffs it, and the bees go all quiet and peaceful. The bees love bourbon. Dooley takes a big gulp and works on forgetting the man in the toaster and the look of surprise on the poor bastard's face. He turns from the bar, and heavy-legs it through the house in search of the bathroom, where he hopes his new roommate will have something for pain. Something faster than bourbon.

Ohhh, the bees warn him. *Ohhh.*

Dooley weaves through room after room until a bathroom appears. It looks like something right out of one of Tina's decorating magazines, all wainscoting and claw-foot tub, tiny soaps and candles. On a hook near the door is a silk bathrobe, the kind Dooley has seen in movies but never actually touched. The whispery fabric makes Dooley want to be dry, to have the silk next to his skin, to feel not just comfort but pleasure again. He wrestles to get loose from his wet clothes and nearly takes a header into the sparkling tub. Free of the soggy mess, his skin throbs with gratitude as he slides on the robe. It smells like his grandfather's talcum, like a life of clarity and ease. Already things are looking up.

When Dooley turns around, there on the double vanity is a mother lode of relief. According to the label on the bottle of OxyContin, Jeffrey Mathers has chronic back pain. Dooley shakes a 20 tab into his palm. He doesn't have back pain, he's just sad, and he needs the little chemical erasers to clear the unpleasant pictures in his mind. When the erasers wear off, Dooley knows, when the picture fills in again, a hot, idling sadness will be parked right in the middle of his chest. There's not one place he will ever go without it again.

Dooley bends down and digs in the pocket of his soaked pants until his blistered fingers snag on his Swiss Army knife. Placing the tab of Oxy on Jeffrey's stone countertop, he uses the knife to shave the time-release coating off. He needs some relief, and he needs it now. Once he's removed the coating, Dooley pops the pill into his mouth and chews slowly, dropping the knife and a few extra tablets into the robe's pocket. He weds the drug to some bourbon and sends them both on a honeymoon to his stomach. He waits to see if he'll throw them up, but he doesn't. He's committed.

He puts the bottle of medicine back where he got it. In the bathroom mirror, a tired man with a soon-to-be-ex-wife stares at Dooley like he knows him. The man's baby is gone, gone for good, straight up to heaven where all children go when their little hearts explode. What the man's wife said is true: "You're going to hell," Dooley informs the man in the mirror. "Directly to fucking hell."

He grabs his tumbler of bourbon and leaves the bathroom wearing the fine silk robe. Jeffrey's house is like a maze, and Dooley stumbles through it in search of the living room. For a while, he goes in circles, as though he's trying to exit a complicated cloverleaf of interstate highway. When he finally makes a successful turnoff into a large living area, he sits down in a Sharper Image massage chair, the kind he's often sat in while Tina shopped at the mall.

The room is spinning, and he closes his eyes against the whirling scenery and presses his face against the contoured surface of the chair, whose fabric feels like skin, but not delicate skin, not like a baby's cheek or the inside of a woman's thigh. Not like the burned tips of Dooley's own fingers. He gives one of the pink lozenges of blister a lick. It tastes like stupidity.

When he opens his eyes, light is beaming in through the leaded glass of the front door, and it hovers over Dooley's head like the old spotlight at Don Quixote's where his band used to play. The bright shaft looks dense enough to slow him down or stop him, but he can put his blistered hand right through it, like a ghost entering another dimension. The bees hate it. They start up on Dooley so loud that he pulls the Oxy tabs from the pocket of his robe and stuffs one in each ear then tosses another one in his mouth, where he grinds it with his teeth and gives it enough bourbon to get it where it's going fast.

The room's light seems attached to a dimmer somewhere, and color fades from everything except for a bright flashing on the periphery. The pulsing at the edge of the room hums. *Ohhh, ohhh, ohhh.* It's made of bees.

Dooley can't think of what else to give them.

He roots around for his Swiss Army knife, and it's there in the robe's pocket, exactly where it's supposed to be. A sign, Dooley thinks. He never finished clipping his toenails the day Tina laid the bad news on him, the day everything turned upside down.

Now the nail on his big toe is long, freakishly long, like you'd see on a dead man if you dug him up after a couple of years. It occurs to Dooley that maybe this is the source of the bees' worry. He pulls his foot up to cut the nail with his knife's little clipper. Several times he hauls it up onto the edge of the chair. Each time he gets it close enough to work on, though, he loses his grip, and the whole operation just falls apart.

What Was Left

On the way home, Pudge scoots off the sidewalk to the street, where his neighbors' cars line the curb. He stands behind the truck everyone calls Big Red, waits for a swarm of schoolkids to cross up at the corner. He doesn't need any comments from the rugrats. Once they're gone, he braces himself against the truck's tailgate, leans over and heaves until just before his eyes pop out. He lifts his spinning head, wipes his mouth. Studies a muscular man dismounting from a white truck. LAFLEUR'S WINDSHIELD MAGIC is stamped on the door like a dare. *Do you believe in magic?*

This Lafleur guy glides over to Big Red and lays a chamois cloth on the hood and a little toolbox on top of the chamois. Pudge fakes a steady walk to the front of the truck and leans against an oak tree next to the passenger-side door. There's a hole in the windshield. Bright cracks filled with light blast out from its dark center, flash in the low morning sun. It tears straight through Pudge's eye and sets fire to his brain. He's still drunk from last night. But not drunk enough.

"How'd you get to doing this?" Pudge asks Lafleur, whose triceps moves up and down like a jaw chewing as he mashes some kind of paste into the dark mouth of the crack. The guy looks across the hood at Pudge and then back at the windshield. Pudge fires up a cigarette and nods. Lafleur keeps quiet. Pudge inhales, holds the hot smoke in his lungs. Waits. Nothing. He'd been smoking a joint a minute ago, hadn't he? Or maybe that was yesterday. Or earlier this morning. In any case, he has the munchies now. He hitches up his pants. It'd be nice to get back a little of the weight he lost. Just enough to give his pants some traction.

This Lafleur guy looks familiar, but after a certain age, everyone does. It might be they went to school together. Pudge was the fat kid with the drunk parents. No point bringing that up. He takes the cigarette from his mouth and looks at it. It looks right, but it tastes like shit, and Pudge replaces it with a stick of gum. A couple of his teeth holler about the sugar, but the chewing drowns out the noise soon enough. To steady himself, he imagines bacon. A whole plate of bacon.

Once his head's right, Pudge pulls away from the tree and leans on the hood of the truck. Used to be you had to just live with it when your windshield got a crack. But now these guys can make the cracks disappear, and people are willing to pay cash money for it. "I mean," Pudge says to Lafleur, who still hasn't opened his mouth, "I was thinking about getting into a new line of work. You know, a career change. I just thought to myself that fixing windshields looks to be pretty interesting."

"It takes a certain touch," Lafleur says. He digs a small key from the pocket of his chinos. Pudge watches the key fit perfectly into the lock of Lafleur's plastic toolbox. "It looks easy," Lafleur says in a warning kind of tone, "but it takes a certain touch."

"Well, I'm pretty good with my hands," Pudge says, swallowing a belch.

Lafleur looks up at Pudge and then back at his work. Says nothing. The man knows how to concentrate, that's for sure.

Pudge imagines himself mashing secret sauce into windshield cracks. He'll get a shirt with his name on the front and the name of his business on the back. He can call it anything. Working with his hands like that, he'll have to get some suspenders. Won't be time to haul at his pants all day, and a belt just squeezes the life out of you. He'll get a cell phone and an office, maybe. *Funniest thing happened at the office yesterday . . .* Pudge will have to fix his truck and hire a helper to drive it until he can get his DWI straightened out. And the helper can handle the paper end of things because paper tends to get away from Pudge. The main thing is he'll be legit. A little cash will get him out from under the VA. And he'll give Deysi money to take care of their kid. Maybe then they can all tell Deysi's boyfriend, Junior, *adios.*

Pudge imagines sitting with Luis and telling him the truth at last. I'm your old man, he'll say. Or maybe *your dad.* Deysi calls her father *Papi,* so maybe Luis would like that better. Pudge isn't a deadbeat dad. He's more like an undercover dad. He sees Luis every day, and recently, he's started hanging out with Deysi's boyfriend, who's a jackass, just so he can keep an eye on things. But *Dad?* Deysi told Luis that Dad died in the war a long time ago. Luis is twelve, nearly grown. Why blow it for the kid is what Pudge figures.

He shifts his weight forward on the truck, works his eyebrows around to show Lafleur that he's interested, that he's a quick learner. He tries to breathe through his nose, exhale downwind. There's a bottle of Wild Turkey inside him that hasn't burned off yet. He studies the spider legs of the windshield's crack. A deadly spider the size of Pudge's hand. "That's a big one," he tells the guy. "You'll damn sure need some magic to make that thing disappear."

"That's what I mean about taking a certain touch," Lafleur says, staring hard at the center of the crack. "Some guys would walk away from this one."

Pudge wonders how much it will cost to get his new business started. He's feeling a little drifty, and it might be that he's already asked, so he keeps quiet.

"And you can't teach that," the guy is saying when Pudge tunes back in. "A man has it, or he doesn't." Lafleur screws some kind of suction cup over the crack. "Getting in is kind of steep," he says. "Take fifteen hundred just to get started." Lafleur looks over at Pudge. "Cash."

Pudge is glad he kept quiet and didn't ask about the cost twice. "Well," he says, "that's doable. Completely doable." Pudge sees that he might be able to pull this off after all. "Maybe a little discount for a veteran?" he tries.

Lafleur reaches into his box of tools. "Is that what that limp is about, the war?"

Pudge nods. "Sure is." Not exactly a lie. Almost nothing is exactly a lie.

Lafleur wipes at some paste that dribbled on the glass. "Well, I gotta get fifteen hundred, irregardless," he says.

Pudge tenses up a little at the thought of what all he'll have to do once he's in business for himself. He'll be his own boss, sure, and all the profits will be his, but so will all the headaches. There's bad checks, for one—no, he won't take checks. But there's always the helpers not showing up or showing up loaded. Pudge pulls in a deep breath, hoists his wallet from his back pocket. There's the joint he had going before. He covers it with his thumb. "You got a card?" he asks the man. "I'll have to move some money around before I can get you the whole fifteen hundred, but I'll give you a call tomorrow or the next day. I got a little business venture's about to pay off." Pudge traded a guy some antique coal grates for a set of steel rims, and those sell pretty easy. And he can maybe sell the radio out of his truck, which is up on blocks again.

Pudge takes the guy's card. It's as white as his truck. "Calvin Lafleur," he reads—he'll need cards, too, he guesses—"I'm Pudge Morris." Pudge is careful to wipe his hand on his pants before he offers it for shaking. "When's a good time to call?"

"When you have the money," Calvin Lafleur says, tapping at the cell phone clipped to his belt.

Pudge nods. "All right, then. I'll most definitely give you a call in a day or two." Pudge turns and trips over a tree root. His own feet. A caterpillar. Something.

Later that afternoon, in his room over the Latin American AA, Pudge pulls a tallboy from the refrigerator and sucks down a few swallows. He's got cottonmouth from the joint he finally remembered to get out of his wallet. His black garbage bag of laundry is packed pretty tight, but Pudge is out of quarters. Not enough time to get to the Bubble and run a load anyway. He excavates the bag for a shirt to wear to his party tonight. Pudge's sister, Belinda, tricked him into dinner at their mother's to celebrate his birthday. Pudge hates parties. "You don't hate parties," Belinda informed him. "You have a phobia, and the best way to get over a phobia is to confront it." Belinda teaches psychology at the junior college. There's not much anyone can say that's news to her.

It looks like this might be a good year after all, though. Pretty soon, he'll own his own business and then he'll sit Luis down and tell him what he should've been told a long time ago. My dad's a businessman, Luis will be saying in no time at all. And it'll be true. Luis is a sharp kid, and Pudge can't believe he bought Deysi's story about how his father died in the war. There wasn't any war going on when Luis was born. Maybe they don't study wars in the sixth grade, or maybe Luis doesn't like history. In school, Pudge wasn't much for history, himself. Same thing happening over and over. Who wants to read about all that crap?

Pudge tunnels under his mattress to see if he left one of those Van Heusen button-downs under there. Squeezed between the mattress and the box spring is the best place to keep a crease on those shirts. Belinda gives him one every year, but they tend to disappear on him. He needs to wear one tonight to show his sister that her efforts to civilize him haven't been wasted. "I just need a little seed money to get the business started," he'll tell her. "So I can do better. You know, for Luis." Belinda rakes in a fair bit of coin teaching psychology, so she might be good for some cash. His mother generally gives him a twelve-pack of beer and cash if she has it. Pudge won't get the whole fifteen hundred tonight, but it'll be a start. The important thing is he's got a plan. T minus fifteen hundred and counting.

He checks a few other likely spots for a shirt, but it's no use. All the bullshit Van Heusens have gone off somewhere. Probably to a martini bar Uptown. Pudge goes with his lucky Saints jersey, which he drops into a sink full of soapy water. He shooshes it around in the suds, then blots it with a towel and pops it into the microwave for a quick dry. He watches the jersey spin in the invisible heat waves. It's sleeveless and that might be a problem because Pudge has his name tattooed on his arm, and his sister just hates it. She's always laying her psycho hoo-ha on him about it. Says his nickname, Pudge, has shaped him, tied him irrevocably to the pain of his childhood or some such shit. She always uses ten-dollar words to show off her college education. Anyway, his nickname is the only thing his old man left him, and it's just a name. A person is not a name.

Besides, Pudge isn't even fat anymore, not by a long shot. And he hasn't been since he got out of the Army, which was quite a while back. That was a good time, when he was in the Army. Pudge still wears his dog tags as a reminder of those sunny days. He likes the sound of the thin metal tablets clicking against each other, and how he can read his name, the one he never uses, with his fingertips. It's like the Clayton Morris of the dog tags is someone separate from himself. Someone wise who watches over him. If he hadn't slipped in a rock climb during boot camp, Pudge probably would have gone career military. But they turned him loose because his knees were trashed, and the army won't keep what it can't use.

Now Pudge yanks his jersey out of the microwave and tosses it in the freezer to cool off for a second. The last tallboy in the refrigerator goes in his pocket for the trip. He meant to hold off drinking so he could have his wits about him when he laid out his business plan for Belinda and his mother. But it takes a fair amount of alcohol to enjoy the love of his family.

From the stairwell of his mother's apartment building, Pudge hears a grenade go off. Pots and pans hitting the floor upstairs. Women screaming at each other. His family.

"Where's the casserole I left?" Belinda is yelling.

"How the hell should I know?"

"Because, Mother, I only left it here two days ago, and I told you it was for Pudge's birthday dinner."

"I don't think that was two days ago. Couple weeks more like."

"Oh, Mother!"

Belinda got this "Mother" business from her girlfriend, Carolyn, her *life partner,* who comes from a well-to-do family. They both say *lovely* a lot, too.

When Pudge walks through the door, his mother puts the argument on pause for a few seconds. "Hey there, Sasquatch," she says. Pudge hasn't shaved in a few days.

The arguing goes on for a little more, and then there's just the sound of the TV. The yelling leads right where Pudge knew it would: the casserole's still not there.

"Hey, Mama. Hey, Belinda," Pudge says to the opposite sides of the ring. Belinda answers with her eyebrows, which go up like two black flags. Look out, they say, trouble ahead. Pudge is pretty sure she's doing her count-to-ten-calm-down thing. She's told him that when she's upset, she names the ten Canadian provinces to herself. It calms her. That makes sense. The Canadians are a calm people. Pudge likes to think of bacon when he feels bad.

He goes into the refrigerator for a tallboy, stands there sipping it, waiting for Belinda to get herself right so he can tell her about the windshield-repair business. He counts to ten a couple of times, then pulls out his wallet. "Check this out," he says. He tries to make it sound like he just discovered something fascinating. It's all about tone with his sister.

Belinda squints at the card. "What's Lafleur's Windshield Magic?"

Pudge can feel success coming toward him, and he opens the door to it. "That's a business I'm—"

"Pudge, honey," his mother calls from her big blue chair in the living room. "Bring me a beer, would you?" Pudge can see the back of his mother's nearly bald head. *Wheel of Fortune* is on. His mother loves *Wheel of Fortune.* Pudge looks at Belinda. She's put the card on the counter and gone back to digging in the freezer. She probably thinks she's going to find the birthday casserole. Belinda never can believe that things just disappear. Shirts. Birthday casseroles. All the paperwork of the world.

Pudge gets a beer for his mother. Puts a spare in his pocket.

"*Cashback!*" his mother yells at the TV when a *C* lights up on a ten-space *thing.* "*Crashtest!*" when an *R* follows. "It's *crashtest,* you dumbass! *Crashtest!*"

Pudge sets her beer on the TV tray by her chair. Plops onto the couch.

"Mother, please," Belinda whines from the kitchen. She's got a whine like a beagle howl. Irritates the crap out of Pudge.

"What are we going to eat?" Belinda asks. "Y'all can't just sit in there and get drunk. Tonight is supposed to be about celebrating Pudge."

Pudge looks for evidence of presents. Nothing but three balloons tacked to the wall next to a banner: Happy Birthday! No shirt-sized packages with bows. No envelopes. Money generally comes in an envelope.

"*Crackhead!*" his mother hollers. "Look, Pudge, it's *crackhead*!"

Pudge nods as he gets up and strolls over to the kitchen. "You want anything?" he calls back to his mother.

He pulls up a stool at the island that separates his mother's living room from the kitchen. Belinda has given up on the freezer and moved to the lower cabinets.

"Fucking grease on everything," she complains to no one in particular. Belinda's got two settings: complain and instruct. She doesn't need an audience for either one.

While his sister's face is buried in the cabinet, Pudge takes the opportunity to get up and pull a couple more tallboys from the vegetable bin. His sister's head snaps out of the cabinet, and she shoots him a look. He shrugs at her. Slides the Windshield Magic card off the counter and puts it back in his wallet. He'll have to keep his eye out for a better time.

Back in the living room, his mother throws her hands up in disbelief when a contestant asks to buy a vowel.

"Jesus, Mary and Joseph! What's he wastin his money on vowels for? Any moron can see the word is *crackhead*!"

"See?" she says when two *A*'s appear on the board.

Pudge sets a fresh beer on his mother's TV tray. Before she opens it, she undoes one of the two bobby-pin *X*'s on top of her head. Rewinds a string of hair. Puts the bobby pins back. The twin *X*'s look like giant stitches meant to keep what's left of his mother's mind from spilling out.

"*Crus-ta-cean!*" a man on the game show says like he's reading from the pronunciation guide in a dictionary. The audience goes crazy, and the winner jumps up and down. Punches the air in victory. He's a man about Pudge's age, dressed in a three-piece suit. Got him a military-style haircut. Pudge tightens his ponytail. His hair is going the way of his mother's. It might be he should cut it all off before it gets there.

"*Crustacean*?" his mother snorts. "What kinda dumbass word is *crustacean*?"

Pudge tries to think of a way to get the windshield conversation rolling again.

"Hey," he calls to Belinda, "you want me to pour you some of that wine?" Belinda brought a *lovely* bottle of wine in honor of Pudge's birthday. Pudge and his mother only drink beer. While

Belinda's head is in the cabinet, Pudge knocks back his entire tallboy. There's no way he's going to be able to get through this night without a serious buzz.

"I don't want to drink on an empty stomach, Pudge," Belinda says. She's kneeling next to the cabinets, taking out crusty pots that have no lids. "Somebody's got to keep their wits about them here."

"Why don't we just order pizza?" he suggests. With the food problem solved, he could sit at the table with Belinda and his mother. Lay out his business plan.

"Is pizza your idea of a birthday dinner?" Belinda barks. She gets up from the floor. "I'll make you a list for the grocery store."

What Pudge wouldn't give to be able to kneel like that and get up again. Belinda looks down at the circles of filth on her knees and heaves a *Sweet Jesus!*

"You go pick up a few things," she tells Pudge, poking her head into the moldy heart of the refrigerator, "and I'll make you a proper birthday dinner." Spoiled food flies out of the refrigerator like gravel behind a spinning wheel. Pudge moves away from the garbage can.

"Pizza's good . . ." he says.

"Pudge?"

"Well, I'm on my bike."

Belinda pulls her head out of the refrigerator and does a quick study of Pudge's face. "No reason you can't take my car, though, huh?"

Offering her car is a trick, Pudge knows. Belinda has somehow found out about Pudge's most recent DWI, and now she's trying to trick him into confessing. He turns back toward the TV and watches the winner climb into his brand-new Chrysler. For a few seconds Pudge tries to imagine what it must feel like to sit in a new car. Everyone cheering for you. And there's your wife and kids jumping up and down in the clothes they bought especially for this moment.

"Okay then," he says, "gimme the damn keys."

"How many beers have you had?"

"Look, do you want me to go, or not?"

"Not if you're drunk. You can't afford to get another DWI."

She's onto him, all right.

Pudge retreats to the living room. "Well, let me know when you decide what I need to do." He pulls the spare beer from his pocket and hands it to his mother so Belinda can see it's not for him.

"Belinda, let your brother alone, would you?" In her chair, their mother twists her torso toward the kitchen. "Just give it a damn rest."

"Nobody would have to go to the store, Mother, if you hadn't eaten the fucking birthday dinner."

This malarkey could go on all night. "Hey," Pudge says with his fascinating-discovery tone. "Did I tell y'all about the windshield repair business that—"

"I never ate any birthday dinner," his mother huffs at Belinda.

Belinda slams the refrigerator door. She puts one hand on her hip. Jabs a finger in their mother's direction. "Right, Mother," she squeezes through clenched teeth, "the casserole just disappeared."

Pudge's mother rocks her upper body in an effort to rise from her chair. Once she's up, the extra momentum shoots her straight into the coffee table. She grabs at her shin. "Goddammit!" The remote goes flying off the arm of the chair and tips over her fresh beer on the TV tray. Pudge gets to the beverage before much is lost, mops the spill with the hem of his jersey, then guzzles the remains. Nobody's looking at him now.

"You always did have a smart mouth," his mother hollers. She staggers toward the kitchen, pecks at the air in front of Belinda with two fingers scissored around a cigarette. "Your problem, missy, is you don't know when to shut it."

Belinda and their mother have been having this exact same fight pretty much since Belinda could talk. Pudge has never understood how the same words can make them just as mad every single time. It's one of the things that depresses him about life. He turns his attention to the TV and tunes out the fight.

While watching a girl cut up avocados on the TV, Pudge decides he should call Deysi. He should tell her . . . well, he never knows what to tell Deysi. He could talk to her back in the day, but not anymore. That Deysi's gone. Back in the day, she'd sit on Pudge's lap. Reach in his shirt and grab his dog tags. She'd run her finger over them and say his name, *Clay-tone,* with a Spanish accent. She said his name like she knew what all Clayton Morris could do in life. If he could call that Deysi, that back-in-the-day Deysi, he'd say, "Get ready, girl. Clayton Morris is gonna rock your world."

"Pudge, honey," his mother calls from the kitchen table. How long has she been over there? "Come look at this." Her voice sounds tired, froggy, like she's been crying.

Pudge looks over to where his mother and his sister have settled in at the table. There's a photo album between them. It's time for the meaningful birthday moment. Nothing says meaningful to Belinda like pictures from Pudge's childhood.

There wouldn't be a better present in the world than never having to look into the piggy eyes of his younger self. But that's not the way the happy birthday dinner goes.

"This is him and your father, that bastard," his mother's saying when Pudge gets to the table. "Wasn't Pudge a cute baby?"

Pudge catches sight of his porky bald baby self balanced on the hood of a car, one hand on his father's shoulder. His father is a greasy teenager whose acne-covered face is pulled up in a sneer in case anyone was wondering what he thought of the whole deal. This teenager, this father, is whittling, and the knife blade is just a hiccup away from the accordion of fat on Pudge's leg.

Belinda pours the last of the special birthday wine into a blue plastic cup. "That's a lovely little outfit he's wearing." She and Pudge's mother lean in to get a better look. No one mentions the obvious; no one says a word about how baby Pudge looks just like a Shar-Pei puppy.

This silent pity makes him thirsty, and Pudge goes to the refrigerator for a beer. No sign of dinner. And still no presents, no envelopes lying around, either. He pulls a couple of twelve-ouncers out of the fridge and then leans on the counter and drinks one down. Pow! He crushes the empty can in the sink. A smile of blood forms where a fold of aluminum slices into his palm.

Pudge's legs shake. He reels away from the sink, wraps his bleeding hand in a stiff dish towel. No telling what all it's mopped up.

"Oh, when was this taken?" his sister asks. There's not a picture in there she hasn't seen fifty times.

"That was . . . well, hell, I can't remember. Pudge? Come look at this thing and tell your sister where you were."

If he doesn't walk over there, Belinda will start in with the beagle howl. No birthday money in that. If he can just get her past the pictures, she might remember about the presents. And then Pudge can pull out Lafleur's card and tell about the business. He straightens himself and slogs through the pile of spoiled food around the trash can.

Even from five feet away he knows what the picture is. So does

Belinda. Everyone in the whole neighborhood knows. Even his mother, but she forgets it over and over. Making Pudge say it is Belinda's way of forcing him to "embrace his pain." That's one of her projects for him, that pain bullshit.

"Looks like a birthday party," he says, trying to keep things light. He closes his eyes, imagines Belinda flipping to some other picture.

"Well, son, we can all see the birthday hats. Whose party was it?"

"What a lovely cake!" Belinda says.

The beer has stopped working. Pudge can feel the sixth grade roaring straight at him. His legs tremble. He wonders if maybe they'll fold, and he'll be spared after all. It would feel good to just collapse, hit his head really hard, maybe even lose his memory.

"Pudge?"

"What?"

"Whose birthday?"

"Spud Dejarnette."

"Spud?" his sister repeats. "Oh, is that the party when . . ."

"What?" his mother asks. "When what?"

"Kinda funny story now," Pudge says. He swirls the remains of his beer. Takes a swallow, but it won't go down his tightened throat.

"Funny? It must have been horrible!" his sister corrects.

"Is that the party when what?" his mother asks. Pudge wonders if she really can't remember or if she's just giving Belinda what she wants.

"You remember Spud, Mother," Belinda says. "The little special needs boy?"

Pudge's mother searches the ceiling for a memory.

"Well, he invited Pudge to his birthday party. Poor old Pudge was so fat back then. Didn't have a friend in the world. Remember?" Belinda takes a sip of birthday wine. "Well, it came time to sing 'Happy Birthday,' and all the kids were around that lovely cake singing. Pudge sneezed right when they got to the 'dear Spud' part. And farted. Loud."

"Holy shit!" his mother says and looks from Pudge to the picture.

"That's not even the worst of it," Belinda says excitedly. "Snot went all over the cake."

All. Over. The. Cake. That's how Belinda says it. His mother shakes her head in disbelief. Pudge doesn't hear what comes next because he's down the stairwell and out on the street before Belinda can move on to his tattoo and the marked-for-life speech that comes after that. He doesn't know how to fight, but he does know how to leave.

Pudge pushes his bike in case his sister is watching, in case he falls. He's jittery and mad and not sure he can ride. Once he's out of sight, he hops on the bike and heads for the Bubble so he can check on Luis before he goes home. A while back, somebody ditched a Beemer across the street from the Laundromat, and that's where Luis hangs out at night. When Pudge turns down Palmyra Street, though, he smashes into the side mirror of Big Red. His dog tags flip up and crack hard against his teeth. Somehow his foot gets caught in the spokes. He slides, palms down, across the cement, the bike attached to his foot.

Why get up, Pudge wonders when the sliding ends. Why not just let the night finish him off? He waits for a car to come along and do just that. The street is dark and empty, and, after a while, Pudge has to admit that there's nothing to do but go on. He sits up, brushes his hands against each other. Street crud rains from his shredded palms. When he tries to stand, his ankle won't support him. It's like he's got a rubber foot down there. A floppy cartoon foot. His right index finger is cocked out at a funny angle. He tries to bend it, but it's like his finger is finished doing what Pudge wants. He starts hopping toward the Laundromat.

He's a little juiced from the adrenaline of his fall. The more he hops, the more juiced he gets, and it's like all his sleeping circuits fire up at once. Every one of them sends his brain the same news: his ankle hurts like a motherfucker.

While his body gets back in touch with itself, his mind bounces around in his skull. Right when he sees the Laundromat, a memory shakes loose in Pudge's brain. There's something about how the snack machine inside is throwing light out into the dark street. All day Pudge has been trying to remember how he knows Lafleur. And now he does. Lafleur used to be engaged to Pudge's friend, Delia, who owns the Laundromat. And now Pudge remembers Lafleur getting Milk Duds from that exact machine. A long-ass time ago. Still, it's a connection, a leg up. Pudge will show Delia the Windshield Magic card. If she says Lafleur is on the up and up, Pudge is going to get busy selling those rims, maybe see if somebody needs him to rewire something. He's good with electricity.

Across the street, the BMW's passenger window is open. Luis is in the back, sound asleep, a miner's light strapped to his head. The batteries must be about gone because there's only a smudge of yellow light left fighting to get out.

Luis has been sleeping in the car. Pudge has to work hard to keep himself from thinking about why. Or what he should do about it. And how. What kind of protection does he have to offer this boy? A beat-up old man with crappy knees, a foot that won't support him, a finger pointing in the wrong direction.

He hops across to the car to get a better look at his son. Luis is pressed into the corner in the back, his hands sandwiched between his face and the glass like he's praying. There's only the dim eye of the kid's headlamp watching over him, and it stares right at Pudge. Pudge eases open the door and rolls the window up against the cool night. That light, he imagines, will burn out soon, and Luis will wake alone in the dark. Pudge slips his hand beneath the chain of his dog tags, lifts them off and hangs them on the rearview mirror. They swing back and forth and then go still.

On the windshield, spider-leg cracks crawl away from a bullet hole on the driver's side. Pudge tries to cover the cracks with his hand, but they run edge to edge across the glass. Some men would walk away from that kind of damage. Some men might not have the touch. But when Pudge gets the tools, he's going to give it a go.

The Invitation

The dream goes like this:

I'm watching Maggie, who's reading downstairs in front of the Bubble's big window. Poetry, probably. The setting sun is throwing Maxfield Parrish light across that corner in the room of mismatched washers and dryers. All my customers are gone, finally, and the door is locked. I'm up in the loft, which is a platform that hovers over the center of the Laundromat, and I'm achy with love for Maggie Kelly. She looks up at me, smiles.

We are twenty. This is our past.

I want to call down to Maggie and say, *Come see*, but at twenty, even in a dream, an outright invitation is still well beyond my ability. Maggie and I have touched only once, just before a near kiss. In the dream, I am filled with the longing of that almost moment.

At the back of the Laundromat, there's a kitchen. The door is closed, but I can see inside it anyway. I watch a drop of water gathering like a revelation at the mouth of the faucet. I feel it strain for release, and I want to see it burst open. Then I remember Maggie. When I turn to check on her, she's right behind me, sitting sideways in a captain's chair. One leg up over the worn arm, facing east. One leg down on the seat, facing west. The wide-open geography of this pose makes me fidget. It steals my words and leaves me standing there, mute and filled with an anxious yearning.

Finally, I think to open my arms to Maggie Kelly, and when I do, she floats, mouth first, right to me. Kissing her is like a dream, like something I'm remembering instead of learning, like a dream within a memory within a dream. My heart pounds us backward to the sofa, which is covered with a cobalt blue sarong. *Que sarong, sarong.*

Maggie and I kiss for a long while and then we talk a little, or not talk, I guess. We have that kind of mind-meld that stands for talking in dreams. Maggie's words are like fingers tracing my naked self—not just my body, my self, my whole self—every word beautiful and perfect. Delia, she says. The sound of my name in her mouth gives me the shivers.

Music, perfectly nuanced, accompanies our every move. Like the talking, the music is mind-meld dream music, and we are its source. The back-and-forth of our wills. Notes rise from the heat of us, converge in the air around us. We are made of music. And not just the sweet strings of the violin and the soulful cello. Not just the bold *ta-da* of horns. No. We are the cowbell of the misstep, too. We lose our footing, and it jangles. Hilarious.

And then we're fucking, Maggie Kelly and I. We are lighter than air, floating, euphoric. Even in our weightless state, we're able to get just the right amount of purchase for what we're doing. You, I say to Maggie. One word. The rest of what I mean comes pouring out of my chest, and we ride the wave of it. We circle like seals in water.

I got one more trick up my sleeve, Maggie says, not in words but in pulses, a series of clicks that run up and down my spine.

Downstairs, the glow of the snack machine's light looks like a distant sun just about to rise. It beams with the perfect happiness of being wanted.

Suddenly, the Laundromat's doorbell is ringing. I don't intend to answer it, but then I find myself padding across the cool tiles toward the door. The snack machine's light flickers like a flashback. When I reach to turn the deadbolt, my hand leaves tracers in the air.

I open the door to the smell of Chinese food. "Just say what you want," a delivery guy tells me. Does he mean *say what I want to say* or *say what it is that I want*? I always hear more questions than are being asked. "Just say what you want," he repeats. Emphatic, but not impatient.

It's my fiancé, Calvin, there on the other side of the threshold.

Maggie wakes and sleeps like an animal—quickly, with almost no warning. I want to wake her up now. Is that a trick up your sleeve, I want to whisper in her ear, or are you just glad to see me? When Maggie does wake up, there's going to be a discussion about coffee. This is not a dream. We're not twenty anymore. Not for a long time now.

"You," Maggie murmurs without opening her eyes. *You* is a term of affection between us. Here it probably means it's my turn to get coffee, though. The muscles in her face slacken as she wakes. She's a perfect extrovert, more relaxed when she's conscious and talking than when she's asleep, her thoughts trapped behind the exit of her mouth.

I leave Maggie in the bed, get up and brush my hair. Before I reach the stairs, the doorbell rings. Saturday morning. Probably someone selling religion. Or a crack-addled scammer, maybe, who will claim to live just down the block. He'll ask for seven dollars to get a cab to see his mother who's been rushed to Charity Hospital.

I ignore the bell.

It rings again and there's knocking. I ignore it. The bell again. More knocking. I feel my dream coming back to me as I head down the stairs.

"Coffee!" Maggie yells as I go.

The persistence of the knocking and ringing says crackhead, and I ready myself to be as hard and rude as I know how. I release the deadbolt on the big door and yank it open to find a bag of doughnuts suspended from a hand. My brother curls into the doorway.

"Hold your fire!" Dooley mock-yells and walks in with the doughnuts in front of him for protection.

"I'm going to need some coffee," I warn, taking the doughnuts from my little brother, who is tall and gangly and still crackling with energy from his gig last night, maybe from other things, too. He's wearing a porkpie hat, an undershirt that shows off his ropy, guitar-playing muscles, a tattoo that asks, *Where y@?*

"You want beer or coffee?"

"You got a root beer?" Dooley follows me back to the kitchen, his hand already reaching for a doughnut in the bag I'm carrying. He hasn't been home yet, so he still smells like a bar, like beer sweat, and I sniff at a canister of coffee to block out the stink. At the table, he stretches his long legs out and bites into a neon-sprinkled doughnut.

"You eat like a teenager," I say and flip his hat off his head. His kinky blond hair, our dark skin and light eyes, they tell the story of the French and the Africans, the Scots and the Irish who struggle for ascendance in our DNA. It's the story of most everyone who's from Gremillion, Louisiana, which is where we grew up.

"I got the invitations," Dooley announces proudly and pulls a stack of cards from his messenger bag.

IT'S OUR ANNIVERSARY! the cards blare in forty-eight-point type.

"Uhn-uh. No-o-o," I say. I pick up the stack of cards and hand them back to Dooley. "Not going to happen, Doo."

Dooley's boyish face darkens in disappointment. He's a grown man, but he still has the dire facial expressions of a child. "But they're all printed up," he points out.

"Put them in the bag and take them back where you got them."

"No can do, señorita. That's between you and the missus." Dooley shoves another doughnut in his mouth, chugs root beer, thumbs through an *Offbeat* he's pulled from his bag.

"Fine." I stomp the pedal of the garbage can, and its hungry mouth opens and swallows the invitations in a single gulp. I go back to making coffee. "I told Maggie we could *discuss* having an anniversary party," I say to Dooley. "I did not agree to anything, most especially not those loud-ass invitations."

Behind us, the stairs creak. Maggie. The scene triggers a feeling of déjà vu. The dream of our past, this sleepy lost feeling, the ringing doorbell. My well-worn love comes down the stairs, tying the sash of her killer blue kimono. This is also part of the déjà vu.

"Dooley!" Maggie chirps. "Let's make omelets."

On Monday, Maggie has the evening shift at the Laundromat, so she doesn't come in until noon. I've been here since nine. She sits out front chatting with folks while they do their laundry. I go in the back to fold clothes and wrap them in brown paper for our pickup service. Before I get too far into things, I sneak around the side of the Bubble and hide behind the panel of our defunct pay phone so I can have a smoke where Maggie won't catch me. Ten bucks a bust, that's the deal we made. The notion that I might get caught makes me smoke really fast, which is the opposite of relaxing and harder to do than it looks. I do it several times a day anyway.

Across the street, a neighborhood kid, Luis, holds up ten fingers to show that I'm busted. Maggie has enlisted him as an informant. "You could pay me five dollars when I catch you," he suggests. "Then you could smoke two times for the same amount."

I say, "That would defeat the purpose," and he just shakes his smooth little head.

"Seem like if you gotta give Miss Maggie ten and you could give me five not to tell Miss Maggie, you could come out way ahead."

"That's a different deal, Luis," I tell him. "That's extortion." Luis is only twelve, but he's the kind of boy who knows what extortion is without knowing the definition of the word.

"Yeah, but it's only five bucks," he says and ducks into the abandoned BMW that's parked across the street.

Cars arrive and disappear on Palmyra Street all the time. This one's got a flat tire, a bullet hole in the windshield—it's a magnet for trouble. Luis has made it his private clubhouse.

I finish my cigarette, wave to Luis, who's pretending to drive. "Better buckle up," I yell across the street, and then go back to my folding inside.

One morning Maggie offers to paint my toenails. With our anniversary coming up, romantic gestures from our past are enjoying a reprise. I know she's after something when she makes the offer, but she's good with that tiny brush, so I accept.

Halfway through: "Why can't we have an anniversary party?"

I say, "It was the fucking party planning that broke us up before."

"Weird," Maggie muses. "I thought it was infidelity and messed-up priorities."

"You know what I mean."

"It'll be fun," Maggie assures me. "Don't you want to celebrate the abomination of our homo love, our unholy, unblessed union?"

"Ah, the dark perversion of it all," I say. "Tempting. But I think *the love that dare not speak its name* should keep quiet just now."

Last year, just about this time, we split up briefly, right in the middle of planning an anniversary party. The party was too soon after Maggie's affair. I thought we could put a happy face on things and just move on. That's how I am, always thinking I can do things that are the opposite of how I feel. But sometimes you have to say yes before you feel yes. Sometimes you have to suck it up and be brave. But then again, sometimes you have to pay attention to how you feel. It's never clear to me which moment I'm in when I'm in it.

Maggie slips cotton between the toes of my left foot without breaking eye contact. A shiver of lust runs through me. "Okay," I tell her. She's still looking me right in the eye the way she does when she's waiting for me to talk myself into or out of something.

"But we're not calling it anything. It's just a regular party at the Bubble."

At a regular party nobody's waiting to hear your recipe for success. No one says anything that makes you feel like a fake, that makes you want to set the record straight. At a regular party there's almost no chance that you will have a few cocktails and say, *Twenty years? Not exactly. We broke up for a while after the affair.*

"And I mean it about the regular party thing," I tell Maggie. "I don't want you springing any announcements on me or letting someone give a special toast."

"Fair enough," Maggie concedes and goes back to her painting. "You're in charge of the invitations, though."

"The other ones had the A-word, Maggie. Right on the front."

"So make new ones is all I'm saying."

"Why can't we just stick a who-what-when-where in the front window of the Bubble? Everyone we want to invite is going to walk by there sooner or later."

"Because, Delia," Maggie explains as she works paint onto my nails, "people like to know they're wanted, that their invitation isn't based on proximity, on happenstance."

"No need to dog proximity," I point out, looking from Maggie down to the cotton between my toes. My nails have begun to bloom like berries in the snow, one, then another, then another.

Sex isn't love, Maggie told me, when she was trying to convince me that what she'd done with another woman hadn't meant a thing. "One stupid moment," she told me. "Just one!" She wanted me to stop being mad. She wanted to stop feeling guilty. Who wouldn't? "It's you I love," she kept saying. Sex isn't love. I know that. But just like everything else I know, it's taking a long time for my feelings to catch up to it.

Three weeks before our anniversary, I'm in the back room of the Laundromat. It's nice there. I like the folding, the brown paper packages with their still-warm contents. I like not having to jolly people out of the neighborhood disputes they regularly bring inside. Shut the fuck up or take it out to the street. That's my approach. Or I pull up my bangs and aim the old burn scar on my forehead at whichever kids seem bent on wrecking the place. I've told them it's an evil eye, and they're afraid of it. Soon enough they'll learn that it's the scars you can't see that do the most harm.

Maggie's solutions are more elegant, more entertaining. "Show me your fight face," she'll say, adjusting the lens of her camera. Maggie has a way of charming even the hardest characters. She'll say, "Imagine a '66 Mustang," and make the hardest man's face fill with pleasure. She exhausts their bullshit with her excitement, posing and reposing the "subjects" who come back every day to see if she's hung their picture up yet. They don't come back to fight. They come to be photographed. People just want to be seen, Maggie's always saying. That's what the fighting's about. I don't necessarily care what the fighting's about. I just don't want it inside my Laundromat. Which, of course, is half Maggie's now. After the affair, she quit her executive job and bought into the Laundromat so she and I could be together more, the way we talked about. It's all on paper now, me and Maggie together, the closest we're likely to get to being married in this country.

I've almost finished my folding and wrapping when Maggie comes in and hops up on the counter. "Dooley can play for the party," she tells me, "and he said a couple of the other guys in the band will probably be up for it."

I haven't done a single thing to make this party happen, but it keeps gathering strength anyway. I tell myself to be brave, but the thought of all those balloons, the brightly colored streamers and lanterns. All that attention aimed at me and Maggie. It's too soon. And I'm worried that it will always be too soon.

Maggie checks the counter for evidence that I've been working on the invitation. "How's it coming?" she asks, looking from a stack of towels on the counter to a solitary vase of yellow hibiscus on the table.

"How is what coming?" I ask. I'm being a jackass. I know that.

Maggie nudges me in the hip with her foot. "You realize that you're not going to wear me down with your indifference, right?"

"It's not indifference I was going for," I point out. "I hoped you'd be discouraged by my complete opposition."

"You said you were fine with having a party as long as we didn't make any big announcements. As long as we didn't make it a *thing*."

"I did not say I was *fine*. I said *okay*. *Okay* is made up of tiny molecules of ambivalence, Maggie. It's the opposite of *fine*."

Maggie hops off the counter, backs me up to the wall, makes me look her right in her eyes. "You want to take this step, Delia. You want to let the past go and be happy about our anniversary. And you want other people to be happy about it, too. I know you."

"You're *starting* to know me," I tell her. That's a thing we say to each other when we don't think our complexity is being fully appreciated: *You're starting to know me.* "Twenty years is nothing," I say. "Twenty years is still casual sex."

"Ha!" Maggie laughs and backs away a little. "I know you. You need to drag your feet when you're afraid, and I need someone to resist my efforts. And that," she says, kissing me, "makes us perfect for each other."

"I'm not afraid," I say to Maggie's back as she's leaving.

"You are," she calls over her shoulder. "And you've been smoking, too. But I know you. You'll pull it together."

"I'm still sorry," Maggie said every morning for months after we got back together. I was still mad, still hurt or worried, or I don't know what. What I did know was that I didn't want her waiting around for the blessing of my forgiveness. I didn't want it to be up to me to switch the light back on in our dark time. "Quit saying that," I finally told her one morning, and she did. But she still hasn't stopped waiting for a sign, a signal that the bad times are officially over.

The next time I go out for a smoke, my friend, Pudge, comes wobbling around the corner of the building. He sprained his ankle, or broke it, and he's made a cane out of a piece of galvanized pipe. He clangs down the sidewalk with it, checks the pay phone for change, then leans against the wall next to me.

"He's been sleeping in there," I say, jutting my chin toward Luis, who's still in the BMW. "And I don't know how he got them, but I saw your dog tags hanging on the rearview mirror the other day."

Pudge puts his hand to his chest where his dog tags have hung ever since I've known him. He nods and exhales, his breath flammable. "I know," he sighs. "I know." He lights a cigarette and looks away from the street. Luis is his son, though Pudge hasn't gotten around to telling the boy. "Deysi told him his father died in the war," Pudge blurted out late one night, years ago, long after we'd all heard that story from Deysi herself. Then he cried until he passed out drunk right about where we're standing now.

I'm pretty sure Deysi has slipped down the rabbit hole of meth. Her boyfriend, Junior, is the neighborhood boss, and he has somehow sidestepped the efforts of Child Protective Services, which I've called twice. I'm not sure CPS would get Luis into a better situation anyway. Shouldn't we all take care of him until Deysi can?

"Pudge," I say. "I wish I could get him to sleep in the back." I've turned the back storage shed into a guest room with all the amenities, including a door that can be bolted from the inside.

"Did you tell him the room is for him?"

"You know how Luis is," I say. "You can't give him anything without him thinking it's a trick. He knows I leave it unlocked."

"Well, maybe tell him not to go in there. You know, like reverse psychology."

I try to think of what reverse psychology would get Pudge to pull himself together and take charge of his own son. "Hmm," I say.

Out of the blue, he asks, "What was that old boy's name that you were engaged to back in the day?"

"Calvin?"

Pudge pulls a card out of his wallet. *Lafleur's Windshield Magic* is printed on it in an elaborate, raised script. Calvin Lafleur, Proprietor, it proclaims. Before Calvin quit Spanky's Automotive, Maggie and I used to run into him and his wife, Janet, at the po-boy shop, which is right behind Spanky's. I haven't seen either of them now in a couple of years. "Where'd you get this?"

"Calvin Lafleur. He was fixing a windshield down the street." Pudge turns back toward the BMW, checks on Luis, uses the side of the building to roll the ashes on the end of his cigarette into a neat cone. "He does good work," Pudge says, meaning Calvin, I guess. "Said he could teach me the business."

This last part sounds improbable. One look at Pudge and Calvin would write him off. "Did he remember you?" I ask. My loft dream floats up to my conscious mind, and I am tempted to believe that I have pulled Calvin into my present tense with just a dream.

Pudge tells me that Calvin didn't seem to remember him. "I'll tell you what, though," he adds, "I didn't remember him right off, either." He strums the greasy strings of hair on top of his head. "But then I was just walking down the street the other night, and I thought, I know how I know him. That's Delia's old fiancé."

Fiancé. I haven't thought about Calvin that way in a long time. I cheated on my fiancé because I was in love with Maggie Kelly. I never told Calvin that. We split up not long after Maggie and I made music up in the loft that first time.

"You got an interest in that kind of thing, Pudge? Fixing windshields?"

"I-I gotta get him away from Junior," Pudge sputters, nodding toward Luis.

"What's that got to do with windshields?"

"Money, Delia. Real money that I could give to Deysi. Then she can tell Junior *adios.*" He shakes his head no then nods to himself like he's listening to both sides of an argument. "Well, that's not right, sleeping in a car," he says indignantly. "And Deysi's not gonna do anything. I mean, she can't right now, you know?"

I do know. But I wonder what makes him think Deysi wouldn't just hand the money over to Junior to buy the smoke that's causing the problem in the first place. "Maybe time for a paradigm shift," I try. *Paradigm shift* is a phrase Pudge used a lot back in the day. For a while he seemed committed to getting free of his dependence on his piss-poor veteran's benefits, which were constantly being cut or arriving late or not at all. *I'll tell you what,* he used to say. *I'm sick of waiting on the VA to get their act together. The only one who can turn this thing around is me. It's time for a paradigm shift.*

Pudge ignores the paradigm thing and goes back to his business plan. "So you think he's on the up-and-up? Calvin's a good guy?"

"Calvin's the best," I assure him.

"Well, then all I gotta do is get the start-up money together, and I'll be good to go." He pauses to see if I'll jump in to volunteer cash. I don't. I never do. I'm pretty sure it's why we've stayed friends so long. Pudge nods his mournful nod. The sharp bones of his face all point toward the cleft in his chin, the telltale chin that's planted on Luis's face as well. Pudge's sunken cheeks make him look forever on the verge of tears. He's told me that he was a fat child, which is hard to believe. He's rail thin, with a high beer belly, no ass to speak of, his pants perpetually slipping toward his ankles.

While Pudge is waiting to be sure I'm not going to chip in start-up money for his business, he turns his attention to Luis. The boy has strapped a miner's light on his head, and he's flipping through the green catechism book I found stuffed under the front seat of the BMW one day when I was checking the car for drugs, for needles, for anything that might hurt Luis.

Without looking away from Luis, Pudge says, "Maggie told me you're working pretty hard against having a party for your anniversary."

"An anniversary party is just asking for it," I tell him.

"Asking for what?"

"For trouble, Pudge. Remember last time?"

"Or maybe," Pudge says, "maybe you're yanking Maggie's chain."

I take a long drag and tip my head back to release a prayerful smoke signal, three rings floating up to heaven: Jesus, Mary and Joseph. "Yanking her chain? I'm not yanking her chain," I tell Pudge. "What does that even mean?"

"It means that if Maggie thinks this anniversary party is a sign that everything's okay, and everything's *not* okay, Delia's gonna keep the party from happening instead of saying everything's not okay. 'Maybe I'm going to make those invitations, and maybe I'm not.' 'Maybe I'll send them out in time, maybe I won't.' 'Maybe I'm over what you did, maybe I'm not.' "

"That's some logic you got there." I pick at a chip of paint on the side of the building, exposing bare wood. Layers and layers of old lead paint. I squeeze the little chunk of poison between my fingers. "What you just said there? That doesn't make a lick of sense. That is not how Maggie and I work."

"Yeah, I know. You and Maggie have been to therapy, and now you talk through your differences. Now you're all mature about what's eating you." Pudge shakes his head side to side. "You can't shit me, Delia Delahoussaye. You think this party is some kind of big sign that you've moved on, and you're not sure if you're ready to be over it entirely."

"Uh, headline: I've been over it, Pudge. It's been over. We've already moved on."

"Then why haven't you sent out the invitations yet?"

"Why are you so worried about what I'm doing or not doing?"

"Hmm," Pudge says, payback for hmm-ing him earlier. He puts

his cigarette out on the bottom of his shoe and drops the butt into his pocket. Lights two more and hands one to me.

After that, we smoke quietly. It's a comfortable silence. Except for the very obvious, Pudge is my perfect mate.

While the sky was still falling after our last anniversary, after our breakup, our separation, my brother, Dooley, had an anniversary of his own. Years before, he parked his truck outside a baby boutique and left his daughter sleeping in the crappy car seat he hoped to replace with one he'd seen in the window of the store. Just a spontaneous decision. He could've driven on home. He could've gotten that car seat another day, but he stopped that day and left his baby in the truck because she needed a nap and had finally fallen asleep. When he came out of the store—*just a few minutes later*, he always emphasizes when he tells the story, which isn't often—his daughter had died of heatstroke. In just a few minutes. And last year, on the tenth anniversary of that awful day, Dooley went into a tailspin and ended up on the psych ward at Charity.

It was Maggie I called first. It was Maggie who sat with me, who sat with Dooley, who took a leave of absence from her job to take care of the Laundromat. She left us only to sleep at the breakup apartment she rented a few streets over from our house.

"Come home," I said to her one night on the phone. "This is stupid. Just come home."

There's real trouble in the world. The kind that can't be fixed. The kind we lie awake keeping vigil against. Love is not trouble. It is all we have to light our days, to bring music to the time we've been given.

When there are only two weeks left before the big day, I still haven't started the invitations. I'm in the Laundromat's big kitchen, folding and wrapping, and Maggie comes in to quiz me. "How's the invitation going?" she asks. Maggie's a patient person, but her tone says she's about had it with me.

"I'm working on it." And maybe I am. It always takes me a while to know what I'm actually up to.

Maggie goes back out front. I follow her. I want to tell her that I'm not sure why I'm dragging my feet. I want to tell her about the conversation I had with Pudge last week. I want to invite her up to the loft so we can make a little music, some soulful cello, the sweet strings of the violin. The *ta-da* of horns. And, since the affair, the inescapable jangle of the cowbell, the misstep. Words have a way of swimming off in the wrong direction, but music is always true. Before I can say any of this, I notice a blank spot on the wall.

"Hey," I say. "Where's the picture of Saravuth?" Saravuth is one of the men whose fight face Maggie has captured and hung on the wall.

"Shot." Maggie sighs. "I gave the picture to his brother to carry at the funeral."

Maggie goes to sit out front, and I stay to stare at the rash of empty spots on the wall. One a month, almost, is how fast the men disappear. There's real trouble in the world.

The day the party is supposed to happen it rains. Hard. Palmyra Street floods quickly and often—ankle deep, shin deep in a rain like this—and I think I might not have to confess after all. If I'm lucky, it'll flood, and Maggie will think that's why no one came.

I told Pudge we were having the party, of course, and Big Luce, his old aunt, who owns the building that the Bubble is in and who serves as the Den Mother of Us All. Dooley's band will come. Enough for a party, I guess. I should've mailed the invitations. I made them, showed them to Maggie, even, but then I dropped the whole stack in a box of comics Pudge put out in the shed for Luis.

Six inches of water has collected in the street, and it gurgles around the bottom of the BMW's tires. I slosh over to check the car's interior and find Luis sound asleep in the backseat. In the front, rainwater drips rhythmically through the bullet hole in the windshield, keeping time to Luis's dreams. When I knock, he jumps up with his fight face on.

"Come on and get some biscuits," I tell him and wade back to the Laundromat.

Maggie is at home. She and Dooley are cooking for the nonexistent party tonight. I'm supposed to be decorating, moving the folding tables around to make room for the dancing. Big Luce came to the Laundromat this morning and brought me biscuits for breakfast, along with a case of lemon ices for the party.

Luis empties half a jar of fig preserves onto a couple of biscuits. High from all the sugar, he zips around the room helping me put up decorations. He stops and points at the newest empty spot on the wall. "Saravuth got a dirt nap."

I say, "He sure did."

"He was a badass, but they still got him anyway."

I want to tell Luis something helpful; I want to say, *I got your back, no matter what.* But having somebody's back is what you do, not what you say. "People don't have to shoot each other to get their point across," I try. I check Luis's face to see if this makes any difference to him. It doesn't seem to. "I mean, you can talk about why you're mad, you know. Work things out," I say. Like Luis and I are on some jacked-up version of *Sesame Street.* When you care about someone, there's no end to the ways you can fail them.

Luis shrugs, climbs up a ladder near the front window and loops one end of the lanterns on a hook put there for just that purpose. He runs upstairs to the loft with the other end and threads it between two balusters. Back and forth, back and forth, he goes between the balusters and the hook over the window until the lanterns fan out in a V that creates a canopy of light between the two places. He looks down to where I'm stuck staring at the empty spot Saravuth has left. "Shootin is just lazy," he announces.

I have no idea what he means by this. Even his tone is hard to figure. I wish Maggie were here. She'd know the right words.

I go in the back and get the big extension cord to connect all the strings of lanterns. When I plug it into its usual place, nothing happens. Then I remember that we overloaded that socket at the last party, and it blew. "Help me pull this out," I say, and we jerk at the snack machine, which no one has cleaned behind since Big Luce had her Laundromat here. The opening reveals years and years of compacted lint and dirt and squashed detergent boxes used to level the machine's feet. There's a child's handmade valentine and an empty bottle of Pop Rouge, which hasn't been available for quite a while. I sweep the mess out and give the plug to Luis, who's small enough to slip right into the gap behind the machine.

"Look at this," I say, pulling the valentine from the pile of trash. A red magic-marker heart contains a child's profession of love: *Crazy for Deysi.* "Did you make this?" I ask Luis.

"That's my mama's name."

The valentine is printed on the kind of paper we wrap the pickup laundry in, but a thicker, sturdier version; like the Pop Rouge, that grade of paper hasn't been around for quite a while. "Did you make this?" I ask again.

"You can't call your mama by her name."

I hand Luis the old valentine, proof of some bygone love. "Bring this to your mama," I tell him. "Girls like to know they're wanted. Even big girls. Especially big girls."

"We're still us," Maggie said, after her suitcases had been emptied, after her clothes once again hung next to mine in the big closet upstairs. Months and months ago, this was.

"We're not," I argued, directing Maggie to the spare bedroom—the punish corner, she called it. "We're all broken to pieces, and we are not still us."

A few hours before the party is supposed to start, Dooley and the guys from the band are setting up at the front of the Laundromat. Maggie and I are in the kitchen emptying chips into bowls, transferring beer from the pantry to the big galvanized washtubs in the next room. There's food for a hundred people here, and I can't stand to think what's going to happen when Maggie finally figures out that I haven't invited anybody. That this is it. Next to Maggie, at the sink, a drop of water swells at the mouth of the spigot. I look away so I don't have to watch it fall.

"Maggie," I say, finally, when she pulls out a warming tray for the barbecued shrimp. She's not looking at me. She thinks I'm going to ask where the rest of the ice is. She thinks she's going to say, Out in the shed, and I'm going to go get it. "Maggie," I say again, and my tone makes her look right at me. "I messed up."

"Did you forget to get more ice?" she asks. "You always do that. It's like you do it on purpose."

"I didn't send the invitations," I say, and Maggie's face tenses almost immediately, the way it does when she's asleep, when she's trying to connect the dots without talking.

"But you showed them to me. They looked great."

"I didn't send them, though."

"Goddammit, Delia." Maggie slams the warming tray onto the counter, jabs the plug into the outlet and turns her back on me. "If you didn't want to have this party, why didn't you just say so?"

"I tried to."

Maggie whips back around to face me. She's puffing her cheeks, trying not to cry.

I should feel like an asshole right about now, but I don't. I feel the gash of the affair opening again, just a little, a tear in my soul that just won't heal. Its presence makes me furious. "I told you I didn't want to have this fucking party. I told you. I told you every way I knew how, Maggie."

"Well, if this is your way of doing a little 'Got you last,' congratulations. I feel gotten." Maggie fires out the back into the courtyard, the screen door banging against the building and then slapping back into the door frame. My face burns with the angry sound of it. I should probably go after her. We should probably try to talk about it, like we learned in therapy. But I don't want to talk. Instead, I finish moving beer from the pantry to the galvanized tubs. Enough beer so that each invited guest can consume a case if she chooses.

For a while, I stay out front setting up a drink station, chatting with Dooley. When I finally go back to the kitchen, I find Maggie sitting on the counter wearing that life-sentence look, the one she's worn like prison stripes since she told me about the affair. And I can't stand it. How in every argument Maggie's a prisoner and I'm the warden. And I can't stand that no one can tell us how long until we'll both be free. I turn to the stove where Dooley has left a big pot of chicken andouille gumbo, a favorite from our childhood. I lift the giant lid and sniff at the contents.

"You want help with that?" Maggie asks, hopping down from the counter.

Blood ricochets through my veins, angry and confused in its familiar channels. I take a deep breath. "I could use some help," I say, careful not to let my voice carry even the tiniest speck of tenderness.

When we get the pot out on the table, Maggie cups my elbow. "I shouldn't have steamrolled you into having this party." This is why it's hard ever to stay mad at Maggie. Unlike me, she's always right there with an apology when she screws up. "I shouldn't have pushed," she says.

"No, you shouldn't have," I snip, even though I'm the jackass here.

"Pudge and Big Luce are coming, right?" she asks. "And Dooley and the band. Luis. That's a party right there."

And that's what does it, Maggie bouncing back like that. That's what always breaks me, makes me soften my heart and try to do right. I always wish I were more like Maggie, that I could actually be quick to let things go, instead of just pretending to be.

I let Maggie pull me to her, and I rest my cheek on her shoulder. "I'm so sorry," I whisper into her neck. "It just felt too soon. And it's driving me crazy how I think I should be over it and then I'm not. I want to be. I do. But I'm not." I lift my head and look at Maggie. "And a part of me," I confess, "a really immature part of me, thought that fucking this up would make us even. And then I'd be over it. But I'm not."

Maggie doesn't say anything. We just cling to one another, swaying at the table near the kitchen, me whispering a mea culpa into the confessional of my beloved's neck.

"Tomorrow's another day, Scarlett," she says at last. "We can start over then. But tonight we eat. Tonight we drink."

I point to the galvanized tubs overflowing with beer. "Tonight we drink a lot."

I'm watching the party from the loft, which makes the whole thing feel like a dream. Fragments of conversation float up to me like messages from a collective unconscious. The strings of bright lanterns inside the Bubble look like highways of happy, blinking light that run straight into a hopeful future. At the front, the snack machine glows, steady, sure.

Someone sent an invitation; that much is clear. The big room is filled and still, like magic, people keep coming. I'd like to believe that what I'm witnessing is a spontaneous will of this crowd to gather here to bear witness to the fact that we are still alive in this hard time. There is real trouble in the world, but there is real magic, too.

Downstairs, Pudge is clean if not sober, and twice now I've seen him whisper something to Dooley in between songs. Before Pudge gets too unsteady, Dooley will let him sing with the band. Pudge has a clear, lugubrious bass voice, one that's not necessarily suited to the high notes of "Danny Boy," which is the only thing he ever sings. He's actually developed a nice arrangement for it, but he always cries halfway through the old-fashioned song. Someone always brings him a beer then. And everyone calls his name, *Pudge! Pudge!* Every time, he laughs, makes fun of himself. *Crying like a goddam titty baby.*

I turn away to check the other side of the room and find Calvin standing at the top of the stairs like some new installment of my loft dream.

We hug, and he pulls me up off the ground. When he sets me down again, he flexes his chest muscles, an old habit.

"I hear you got a new gig repairing windshields," I tell him.

"From Janet?"

"From Pudge." I point to Pudge, who's still hovering near the band, waiting to sing.

"Oh." Calvin gives a sharp whistle. "Yeah. Wow."

"He's actually a good guy, Calvin. If you can help him, I wish you would." I lean with my back against the railing, study the other side of the room. Friends and neighbors everywhere.

Calvin sits in the desk's chair, rolls it this way and that. "Laundromat looks good, Delia. You still like it?"

"I do," I answer, and it's true. My love for the Bubble has never wavered.

Downstairs, Maggie is dancing with Big Luce. The sight of her pulls at me like an instinct. I am meant to love Maggie Kelly, is what it feels like. Behind Maggie and Big Luce, Luis has made a hammock with the hem of his shirt, and he's loading cups of lemon ice into it. He'll sell them out on the street and then come back for more. Which is why Big Luce put them there in the first place. We all try to keep money in Luis's pockets.

Calvin gets hold of the stapler on my desk, and he opens and closes it, shoots staples like a kid, complete with sound effects. *Kshh-kshh-kshh.*

"Hey," I say. "I had a dream about you."

The stapler snaps shut. "Ohhh?"

"Not like that, Calvin. I dreamed you were delivering Chinese food."

Calvin is suppressing a grin. He wants this to be dirty.

"You were delivering Chinese food that I hadn't ordered," I tell him.

"Sometimes the ladies don't know what they want," he says, mugging, "till Calvin brings it to them." He flexes his muscles again.

"Doofus," I say.

Calvin is a man of infinite and completely natural confidence. Any second now, he'll charge downstairs and pick up an instrument and play in the band. Or he'll explain to some guy the very best way to catch a catfish. Or he'll juggle what's left of the lemon ices to great applause. That's how Calvin is made.

I'm surprised then, when, instead of dashing off, he comes over and leans against the rail next to me. Puts his arm across my shoulder like an old war buddy. Calvin is a practical, uncomplicated man, who mostly thinks practical, uncomplicated thoughts. I have always felt safe when I'm next to him.

We stand like that for a while, just watching the party. Before I'm even aware that the words have formed in my mind, they spill out of my mouth. "I cheated on you with Maggie," I admit, twenty years after the fact.

"I know," Calvin says, like I just told him his shoe was untied.

"You knew? Why didn't you say anything?"

"People love who they love, Delia. You and Maggie, anybody could see that was love." Calvin squints, as though looking at something small or faraway. "Me and you? That was just small-town kids sticking together until they found their way."

"Proximity," I say.

"Pretty much." Calvin is looking out the front window to the sidewalk, where his wife is doing a trick with a napkin and two spoons. He smiles. "You always were a good friend, though. Even as kids we had that."

"But what about the cheating? Weren't you mad?"

"Of course I was mad, but I got over it eventually." He nods toward Janet outside. "After a while, I had other things to think about."

There's a break in the music, and we both look down into the crowd.

"I'm going to get a beer," Calvin says. "You want one?"

I follow him downstairs, where everyone's had the chance to get enough alcohol in them to be their shiniest selves. Dooley and the guys launch into some Afro-Cubano, and a man from the neighborhood, a recent arrival from El Salvador, plays a set of *timbales* he brought. Several people start tapping counterpoint on empty beer bottles. Calvin disappears into the crowd, and I look around for Maggie. She's over at the beverage table making a nectar soda for Luis, whose dirty face is lit with adoration.

After the jumpy dancing song, Dooley switches to an acoustic guitar, and Pudge limps up to the microphone.

"He's always been a good singer," I hear behind me. Big Luce. She moves up next to me and hugs me to her sideways. "Congratulations," she whispers, leaning in. Despite myself, I'm happy to hear it. Maggie was right: I did want to take this step.

Luis has gone outside, where he's shaking down several guests for the price of a lemon ice, but he's staring back through the window, keeping watch. Up front, Pudge has closed his eyes, and he's burrowing into the lyrics.

But come ye back when summer's in the meadow
Or when the valley's hushed and white with snow

Any second, his voice will break and the words will take him down. We are all, the whole roomful of us, trying to hold Pudge up with our minds. Everyone wants him to make it.

'Tis I'll be here in sunshine or in shadow
Oh, Danny boy, my Danny boy . . .

It's dark now. Outside, termites—Formosans—hover in clouds near the windows, where they fling themselves against the glass, hungry to get at the blinking lanterns hanging over the crowd. If they could get in, they'd eat the paper shades in a second, but the hot lights would kill them for their greed. Even so, I always imagine that they die happy, having gotten exactly what they wanted.

In the end, Pudge can't finish the song. He cries and has to stop. The crowd murmurs its consolations of *next time,* and *almost had it.* Then Big Luce starts to chant *Pudge! Pudge!* and everyone joins in. Someone brings him a beer. Pudge hitches his pants and rocks into the crowd. Before he gets to the *titty baby* thing, the guy who brought the *timbales* claps him on the shoulder. *"Eso si que es,"* he says. It is what it is.

Just before sunrise, I'm cleaning up the empties and wrapping the leftovers while Maggie makes omelets in the Bubble's old kitchen.

I'm a little jittery, worried that the other shoe is about to drop. I can't imagine that Maggie is just going to let my invitation failure go, that she's not even pissed about it. But she's at the stove humming the theme song to *The Jetsons,* and that's not a song a girl can hum when she's mad.

The smell of the omelets draws the *timbales* guy out of the big industrial dryer, where he's been passed out. I wrap a tortilla around an omelet and send him on his way. Before I close the door, I check the BMW. Empty.

Back inside, I lock up. Maggie and I are alone at last. "Doesn't look like Luis slept in the car," I say.

Maggie is cracking eggs into a glass bowl. She does it with one hand, her fingers cradling the shells. "He slept in the shed," she says.

"Luis is in the shed?" I peek out the back door.

"He was," Maggie calls over her shoulder. "He went home a little while ago."

"But how . . ."

"After Dooley and the band left, Pudge walked out to the BMW and asked Luis if he wouldn't rather crash in the back."

"And Luis just went?"

"Yup."

I've spent so much time thinking about how to keep him from rejecting the offer, it's never occurred to me to just ask Luis if he'd like to stay in the back instead of sleeping in the car.

"You want mushrooms in your omelet?" Maggie asks.

"I reckon."

"I love it when you say 'I reckon.'"

"I know you do," I say, and I kiss the back of her neck. I'm thankful to know what she likes, what makes her happy. To know what she wants from me and how to give it to her. I want to ask about the invitations, if she found out who sent them, but I might be getting a do-over here. I might be getting the chance to give Maggie a do-over, too.

I put the glass mixing bowl in the sink and fill it with water. A drop gathers at the mouth of the leaky faucet. It strains against the opening, and I just stand there waiting. When it finally falls, it breaks open in a fit of shine.

After the omelets, I go up to the loft to get my keys and to double-check for other passed-out party guests. Downstairs, Maggie settles into the window seat to read the cards that people brought us. Strings of lanterns blink vaguely over her head. Even the light from the snack machine is giving way to the pink dawn that's gathering around her as though she is its source.

Up in the loft, my heart pounds with a fierce anniversary love. How is it that we have made it this far? I am drawn to Maggie's light, is how I explain it to myself, and she, mysteriously, is drawn to mine. We might die flinging ourselves at each other. But it might be that we will both burn hotly and happily and thoroughly until there's nothing left of us.

"Maggie," I call down to her. She looks up from the cards, smiles at me, a bright, irresistible smile. "Come see," I say.

St. Luis of Palmyra

Luis eases down the hall to where his mama's door is still closed. She's been crashed in her room since he got home from school. The Krewe of Idiots—that's what Luis calls Junior and his friends—are laid out all around the living room. Junior Palacios is his mama's boyfriend, and he doesn't go anywhere without the Idiots, a group of grown men whose only job in life is to follow Junior around and do whatever he says.

In the hallway, Luis stretches up on tiptoe, watches the living room through a fist-sized hole in the hall door. The Idiots are running their mouths about what all they're fixing to do. Big talk about whose car might be just about to disappear and who shouldn't sit on his porch unless he's looking to take the big nap. What they actually do is, the skinny ones fire up some meth and the fat ones smoke a joint. And then everybody's like, Put it on *America's Most Wanted!* And: Gimme the remote, boy! And: Boy? Boy? Go home and tell your mama you got beat up by a boy! All the yelling cracks

Luis up. It seems like everyone would know by now that the remote has to sit on top of Junior's big fat stomach. If you want to watch TV, you're gonna watch what Junior wants to watch. Why argue? But the Idiots always do. That's what makes them Idiots.

"Deysi, you can get your own ass up," Junior yells to Luis's mama, "or I can come in there and get it up for you. You been home all day and we got jack to eat!"

Luis could point out that Junior ain't been about much today, either, but when he gets in the middle of that kind of stuff, it just makes it worse for his mama, so he usually keeps his mouth shut, goes outside until whatever's coming has been and gone. Sometimes, Junior passes out without having to hit anybody.

Luis opens the hall door, keeps his eyes on his own feet. He scoots along the back edge of the living room, into the kitchen, then out the side door. Junior and the Idiots are like dogs or like those giant flying cockroaches: if you make eye contact with them, they feel like they've got to come after you. Luis doesn't have time for all that mess.

Tomorrow is the sixth-grade science fair, and Luis is pretty sure he's gonna win it because science is his best subject. Science doesn't care how big you are; anyone can make it work, which is good for Luis, who's the smallest kid in his grade. He's gonna do a project that shows what makes a radio run. All he needs is a few parts, and he knows just the place to get them.

Luis karate-kicks his way down the alley next to the house. *Hi-yah!* He's ready to knock the nuts off of anybody hiding there in the dark. When he gets to the back pier of the house, he reaches under and runs his fingers along the sill until he snags his screwdriver, the good one he found outside Spanky's Automotive. It's got LIFETIME GUARANTEE stamped right into the handle.

Somebody dumped a red BMW a little farther down Palmyra Street, across from the Laundromat. Luis has been hanging out in it at night. Making plans. He might take that car straight to California. Take his mama with him and maybe a dog, like a pit bull, the kind with those spooky blue eyes. Then if somebody looked at him wrong, Luis wouldn't say a thing. Wouldn't have to say, Mess with me, and my dog gonna fuck you up. He'd let that bad boy's teeth do all the talking.

Just before he gets to his car, Luis sees Miss Delia, who owns the Bubble, which is what everyone calls the Laundromat. She's leaning against the wall by the old pay phone. He watches her take a hit off her cigarette, tip her head back, and one-two-three-four smoke rings come floating out of her mouth.

It seems like to Luis that if you own a place, you should be able to do whatever you want. When Miss Delia wants to smoke at the Bubble, though, she has to do it on the side of the building that doesn't have any windows because she's supposed to be quitting. Miss Maggie, the other Laundromat lady, gets ten dollars every time she catches Miss Delia with a cigarette. Luis wishes Miss Delia would make that same deal with him. He holds up ten fingers to show her she's been caught. Miss Delia puts the cigarette behind her back and rocks her finger at Luis to say, Nuh-uh. Don't tell.

"You got homework at the library again?" Miss Delia calls across to Luis.

That's a joke they have. Luis's teacher is too lazy to give homework or check it, either one. Whenever Miss Delia asks him what he's up to in the car, though, Luis likes to tell her he's doing homework.

"I'm working on my science project," Luis says, and it sounds just right. Like he could do a project and win the science fair tomorrow, no problem. He points to the BMW. "I'm gonna . . ." Before he gets to the end of the sentence Luis realizes that he can't tell her about the radio project. If she knows he's gonna take the radio from the BMW, she might want to tell him it's wrong. Then she'll watch him to make sure he doesn't take it. And she for sure won't aim her scar at it for him. Taking the radio isn't wrong. It's just the way it is. "I got a secret, supersonic, stealth-bomber project," he says, "and those punks are gonna be sorry they ever thought about trying to be in the science fair with me."

The second he's in the car, Luis sees that the radio, which for sure was there two nights ago, is gone, just gone. He checks the back floorboard where he's been stashing his schoolbooks. Nobody's touched them. Figures. No way he's gonna win the science fair now. Probably somebody's gonna make a poster or some rock candy and win. Which is how the world is. The same losers win everything because the good stuff gets jacked before you can get to it.

Luis reaches under the driver's seat for his new catechism book. Still there. When he told his mama he needed a new book, she just wanted to talk about how money don't grow on trees. Everybody knows money don't grow on trees. Luis wonders why people go on and ask you if you think it does. It gets on his nerves. "Ask Junior for the money," his mama told him, but Luis isn't about asking Junior for anything.

He could've bought a new book with his own money, but he's been saving up for in case he gets confirmed next week. Father Ben said don't count on it. But he also said Luis might be able to pass if he turned in the rest of his assignments. Luis felt like asking Father Ben how was he supposed to turn in his assignments if his book was lost. Priests don't understand regular things, though, so Luis just went on and got a new book off a girl in his class. She doesn't really need a book. She's got her some big, thick glasses. No way you could read a book through those Coke bottles. Besides, girls get confirmed automatically because they're good.

Luis wants to tell Miss Delia about how he might be getting confirmed in case maybe she'll come to the party. People pin money on you at your Confirmation party, and probably Miss Delia's got a lot of it. But maybe not paper money. Sometimes Luis helps her count quarters out of a big bucket in the back room of the Bubble. Maybe she would bring that bucket to his party. She also has this shiny scar on her forehead, and she can aim it at things and make them work right, like broken washing machines and wrong-acting children. Luis wonders if maybe she would use it to bring him good luck for the Confirmation party.

Junior says Confirmation is for suckers, and no way is God gonna let a little liar like Luis get confirmed. He told him flat out no when Luis had mentioned that maybe there should be a party for his Confirmation. He said, Oh no, Louise—Luis hates it when Junior calls him that—we ain't havin all those *cholo*s over here. Luis hadn't even been talking to Junior at the time. He'd been talking to his mama, trying to get her to call his *abuelita* and tell her about the party because his grandmother knows how to get things done.

Abuelita is even smaller than Luis, but she's no saint. She will kick your ass if you cross her, and she's not scared of Junior like Luis's mama is. Which is why she's not invited to the house on Palmyra Street. Luis has to visit her at Hosea House, the old people's home a few blocks away, and that's probably for the best. Whenever Abuelita and Junior get around each other, it's never quiet for long.

The day Luis asked his mama about the party, she just shrugged her shoulders like she does for everything. She won't go against Junior. That's all right. When Luis gets confirmed, he'll be a man.

He and his mama can leave Junior's ass, get in the BMW and go, and God can send Junior whatever he's got coming.

Luis sits up straight in the front seat of the car, stretches himself so he can hang his elbow out the window, then gives the steering wheel some serious attention. *Lookin good.* His feet don't touch the pedals when he sits like this, and Luis worries that he will never be taller than his mama, who is a girl after all. When he flips the visor down, a pair of sunglasses falls into his lap, and he puts them on in the dark car. *Smooth.* Occasionally, Luis goes through Junior's pockets and takes things. Sometimes money, which Junior accused him of doing way before Luis actually started doing it, and sometimes things Luis knows will drive Junior crazy. His sunglasses, for example. Junior can't keep track of things like that, like sunglasses. But money? Well, Luis has several shiny pink scars on his head where hair should grow but won't. If Junior's gonna hit him whether he's done anything or not, Luis figures he might as well take a little payment for it.

He crawls over to the backseat and puts on his miner's light so he can see. Father Ben said if Luis misses this last assignment, he'll for sure get left back and have to get confirmed with the babies in the class behind him. He says there won't be any cheating, either, because cheating is a sin, and God won't stand for any sinning. Luis thinks God needs to make up his damn mind. If cheating is a sin and God loves even sinners, then God loves cheaters, which just goes to show how easy it is to get over on God. Luis guesses if it was just God standing between him and his Confirmation, no problem, but Father Ben don't play.

Write about the saint you most admire, the assignment sheet says. Luis digs around for some paper and finds the math worksheet he was looking for a while back. He erases the numbers, then taps the paper with his pencil for a while to make his thoughts come out. Father Ben likes ink, but that's because Father Ben has a nice fountain pen, and there ain't nobody at the rectory trying to get it away from him.

It takes Luis a couple of hours, but, when he's finished, there aren't any scratch-outs or misspelled words. There's not one thing Father Ben can say against it.

SAINT LUIS OF PALMYRA

The saint I admire is call Saint Luis of Palmyra. Saint Luis live way along time ago. Like before television. The reason I admire him is because he'is a good guitar player. And he dont take no lip. Also because he'is not like those other crazy kinda saints always boo-hoo somebody kilt me for loving Jesus. Even though Saint Luis love Jesus, he just dont talk about it all the time. He keep his stuff private. He just like make music and do some good deeds like if a old lady need to cross the street or something. Also he built that place California where everbody can go and just play music or videos and be on tv. This place is like Heaven and everbody look tight and can play music. Like all kinda music. Saint Luis is a good saint because if somebody hurt him, like a giant, he dont just stand there and ax for more. He would make a plan and smite that giant. He will help himself and his family and not wait around and see if the bad people are stop being bad. Or if Jesus gonna make a miracle out of it. The end.

Luis folds the essay just the way Father Ben likes it and slips it into his catechism book. He kicks back in the seat and puts his feet up in the open window, imagines himself at his Confirmation party in a new suit. All his relatives are there. His jacket is covered in money, and there's Miss Delia with a whole bucket of quarters. Luis hasn't mentioned the party around Junior again because Junior will only let the Krewe of Idiots come to the house. Luis is sure he can get Abuelita to make a party for him, and his other relatives will come if she's there.

Around midnight Luis jerks awake in the backseat when a car drives by, slow, music thumping. He quick rolls to the floorboard in case there's gonna be shooting. After the car passes, he looks out in the street. No one. The Bubble is dark except for the snack machine. It glows like a nightlight for Palmyra Street.

Luis meant to go across before Miss Delia left. After she closes at night, she unlocks that snack machine to put the new stuff in and take the money out, and sometimes she lets Luis pick something to eat or keep some quarters if he helps her put the change in those little paper wrappers.

He gets his catechism book and crosses to look at the snack machine through the Bubble's big window, at 3C, animal cookies, his favorite. If you keep the elephant heads, you can make a wish and toss them over your left shoulder for good luck. If he'd been awake before Miss Delia left, he could've got a whole handful of elephant heads and then maybe he would've found a radio on the way home, like one nobody was using.

When he gets back to his house, it's dark except for the TV light. Luis was hoping Junior would already be passed out, but he's still on the couch, which is Luis's bed. The Idiots are slouched and slumped all around the living room, all of them snoring like it's a contest. One Idiot, the skinny one called Pudge, is laid out in the bathroom doorway like he's been murdered. He's got a big wet spot on the front of his pants that makes Luis want to kick him.

Junior's watching a fight on TV. Got a bottle of Wild Turkey parked on the coffee table, a glass of it wedged between his nuts. Luis hates that, how Junior puts everything where he has to touch his nuts to get at it.

Luis can tell that Junior's been waiting for him. If he doesn't give that fat *cabron* what he wants, he'll just go after Luis's mama, and that's always some hitting. It's better just to do the deal and get it over with. Junior usually falls straight to sleep after, and then everybody can get some rest.

Luis puts his catechism book on the upside-down milk crate by the front door. He's mad about the science project. He should've checked some other cars. Like earlier in the week. Then he could've done that radio thing, no problem. But winning the science fair is for little kids anyway. The prize is just like a ribbon, and they say your name on the intercom at school. Big deal. Passing catechism and getting rid of Junior will be ten times as good as some candy-ass blue ribbon.

Junior's scratching his nuts, following Luis with his eyes. His head jerks on its neck like a sprinkler that can only turn a little at a time. What a moron. He probably couldn't make a science project or pass catechism, either one. Luis tries to picture Junior in a suit and tie or hooking up a radio at the science fair. What a joke.

"What you laughin at, *hijo*?" Junior asks, his eyes going hard all the sudden.

"Nothin."

"Well, either I'm crazy or you're lyin because I just saw you laugh. You see somethin here you think's funny?" Junior fingers the glass between his legs and runs his thumb up his dick. He makes that face at Luis, the one that says come on and don't make any noise.

"No sir. It ain't nothin funny." Luis kneels between Junior's legs, thinks about the bottle on the coffee table. In his mind, he picks it up and smacks Junior over the head, then slits his throat with the jagged broken edge.

Luis is late for school the next morning, and when he walks in, Mrs. Green—Luis calls her the Jolly Green Giant because she's like ten feet tall and got some bad breath on her—says, Boy, you don't get your shit together, there ain't gonna be no junior high for Luis Hernandez. Teachers always say that kind of thing to him, but he hasn't failed one time yet. The Giant says his name like LEW-iss, even though he's told her that's not how it's pronounced. She's too lazy to say a Spanish word, though.

The Giant tries to make science class boring with all her bullshit. She just wants to hang a string in a glass of sugar water and then you got rock candy. Candy is for babies. They've been doing that same experiment since like third grade. Luis wants to do the ones about sound waves, but you need some of those tuning fork things, and that would mean the Giant would have to get off her ass and go find some. No way that's gonna happen. In the book, though, it says if you hit that C fork, then you could hold it next to another C fork, and that one'll start making the C note, too. Without anyone even touching it. It's because they're the same. Things that are the same vibrate when they get next to each other.

All those experiments are way in the back of the book, though. They'll never get to them by the end of the year. They have science three days a week, and that's playtime for the Giant. Time to get that nail polish out.

The science fair is after lunch. Luis eats with his class, but when they go out for recess, he just keeps walking until he's out the gate. He pinched a sandwich for his mama off a girl's plate in the cafeteria. Not the screaming kind of girl, the quiet kind that will just cry but not tell. Grilled cheese is his mama's favorite.

When Luis gets to his house, he stands outside the kitchen door, listening. Quiet can be good. Or it can be trouble.

In his mama's bedroom, she and Junior are asleep on their sides, facing the open doorway, Junior with his pig arm pinning Luis's mama. She's got a brand-new cast that starts right above her knuckles and goes all the way up under her armpit. Luis wouldn't mind poking one of those tuning forks in Junior's eye. Hit another one and make that thing vibrate in his head. Long as you had a tuning fork, that fat *cabron* couldn't come near you.

Luis decides he's gonna get his mama something nice, like a present. He looks around for Junior's wallet. Before he can take a step, though, his mama opens her eyes. Looks right at him. Says don't do it with just a look. It's a scared look, and it vibrates in Luis.

Later that afternoon, after Junior goes to do a little business with the Idiots at the vacant house down the street, Luis sits with his mama. "I won the science fair," he tells her. "They said my name on the intercom. And then the mayor came. He said if we move to California, they got an apartment there for us. Free."

Luis's mama stares out the window like she can't hear him.

"I can stay with you instead of going to catechism," he tells her.

His mama reaches her hand out toward him. "Give me a couple of those." She points to a bottle of Vicodin on the nightstand. When he hands her the pills, she flips them into her mouth, chews them up. Almost right away, she's asleep again.

Catechism is clear across Mid-City at Our Lady of Prompt Succor. Luis has to weave through a bunch of second-graders who are walking home from school. The little knuckleheads keep stopping to look at stuff. Invisible stuff on the sidewalk or in the air or way up their noses. Then: Bam! They all take off running for the corner where two girls are in a fight. There's one left behind, a chubby little boy. He's got a great big cuff turned up on the bottom of his navy blue pants in case he ever gets tall enough to match up with how wide he is. And the kid's wearing the whitest shirt Luis has ever seen. It won't be white for long, though. Gordo's got a bag of cheese puffs, and Luis knows he needs to make his move. A clean shirt will impress Father Ben, who unlike God has the power to keep Luis from making his Confirmation.

Luis does a fast walk, gets in front of the kid, then ducks into an alley.

"Hey, kid," he says when the fat boy walks past.

The boy stops and looks down the alley, his hand moving like a piston, up-down, up-down, from the bag of Cheetos to his mouth. When he sees Luis, he tries to put the bag behind his back, but his fat little arms won't reach.

"I don't want your food, man. I need your help."

"My help?"

"Yeah, I need to borrow your shirt for just a minute."

Luis's shirt is the color of mop water next to this kid's, and he drops it right there in the alley, then unbuttons the other boy's shirt. The kid starts crying. Luis can feel Gordo shaking like a fat-boy tuning fork as he removes the clean white shirt from the kid's roly-poly back. Luis looks away in case the boy's eyes are gonna say don't, in case all that shaking is gonna make him shake, too. Luis imagines that God must be testing him with all these bad feelings. When he gets confirmed, when he's a man in God's sight, then God will realize that Luis did all of this for Jesus, who is love, and maybe He will stop giving him bad feelings.

"All right, now," Luis says, turning toward the street. "You wait here. I'll be right back."

The kid says okay, but in a whisper, like it's a secret. Little kids are so stupid. It's like somebody gave them drugs the way they'll just believe anything.

When Luis's classmates are dismissed to go to confession in church, Father Ben, who's still at his desk filling out Confirmation certificates, tells Luis to hold on just a second. He's got Luis's essay in his hand. "What's this?"

"That's my essay," Luis tells him.

"I know it's your essay, but who was St. Luis of Palmyra? I've never heard of him."

"It's all in there about who he was."

"Well, Luis, why do you think I've never heard of him even though I've been a priest for fifteen years?" Father Ben rolls up the essay into a tube and pops Luis on the head with it, but in a friendly way, not a mean way. Like he just told Luis a joke.

Luis explains to the priest that St. Luis was a new kind of saint they just found out about, even though he lived way a long time ago. St. Luis knew how to handle his business and wouldn't let his whole family get hacked up by some stupid giant. "Saints can't be so lazy anymore," Luis tells Father Ben. "They gotta deal." He points out that all the good people who became the old kind of saints got their heads busted open and then went straight up to Heaven, and that left all the head busters down on Earth.

"Well, yeah," Father Ben says, "I can see how that would be a problem after a while."

Then Father Ben says *but* and stops like he's thinking, so Luis has to stand there and wait to hear what kind of mess is gonna be on the other side of that *but*. Anytime somebody says something good and then says *but,* it's bad news.

When he can't wait any longer, Luis asks, "But what?"

Father Ben opens and closes his mouth, but no words come out. He unrolls the essay and reads down the whole page. "But nothing," he says finally. Luis waits for more, for the part where the priest is gonna say the essay isn't good enough and Luis should try again next year. When Father Ben puts out his hand, Luis is so shocked he just about leaves the priest hanging, but right before it's too late, he shakes it like a full-grown man.

Father Ben smiles at Luis. "Congratulations, my friend. You handled your business, and you passed catechism." Then Father Ben reminds Luis that the bishop will slap him during the Confirmation ceremony Sunday, but he shouldn't hit back. The slap is to remind Luis that he should be ready to suffer, even to die for what is right.

Luis wonders which *right* Father Ben is talking about. It looks to Luis like nobody's ever talking about the same one.

"When you get confirmed, Luis," Father Ben adds, "it means that God is on your side, and having God on your side will give you the strength of a thousand men and the Wisdom of Solomon."

Luis isn't sure what that last part means, but it all sounds good. He closes his eyes and pictures the bishop slapping him. In his mind he doesn't hit back. He can do it; he's sure of it.

Father Ben pulls out a certificate with Luis's name on it and uncaps the fountain pen that Luis once used to strafe a classmate. *Ack-ack-ack-ack!* The pen gun left blue blood splatters on the other boy's shirt. *All units in the vicinity, we got a 189 at Prompt Succor.*

"Have you decided on a Confirmation name?" Father Ben asks.

Luis forgot about this part, about how you have to pick a saint's name to be your Confirmation name, and he lost the list that Father Ben gave everyone a long time ago. He wonders if this is a final test. If he guesses wrong, will Father Ben still pass him? The saint is supposed to protect you, and you're supposed to pick someone you want to be like. "Goliath?" Luis says. Goliath, a name like a pit bull.

"Goliath wasn't a saint, Luis. He was the mean giant who hurt everyone, remember?"

Of course Luis remembers, and he wonders again why all the saints have to be such sissies, why they can't be badasses worth looking up to. Although. It was David who kicked Goliath's ass, even though he was small like Luis, plus he could play one of those old-timey guitars. "Oh, I meant David," Luis says.

"David? Okay. David it is, then."

Luis watches DAVID appear on the page, the straight backs of the two *d*'s like the place you could attach rubber bands and make a slingshot to kill a giant. After the certificate is all filled out, Luis gets in line at the confessional with the other kids. Even though it's just Father Ben in there, Luis worries about what kind of sins to tell, what kind of sins a man has to confess. Finally, he decides to say a little about some stealing, but he doesn't mention any names. He wonders if giving Junior a blow job is a sin if he's doing it to keep Junior off his mama. That's between him and God, Luis decides, and he confesses losing his temper instead. Father Ben gives him five Our Fathers and five Hail Marys as a penance, which is what he gives everyone no matter what they did.

After he's through with his penance, Luis kneels in the pew for a while studying the stained glass where the sun has turned into a spotlight over Jesus' head. It makes Jesus look like he just got a bright idea. That's what Luis needs, an idea about how to keep Junior away from his Confirmation party. Luis could use smiting, maybe. Everybody in the Bible smites their enemies, but usually God will smite them for you if he's on your side.

It doesn't seem right to expect God to do his work for him, but Luis isn't big enough to smite Junior himself or vex him, either, which is another thing God does if you go against Him. Luis decides to ask God for an idea about what to do. But just an idea because a man handles his business. He's pretty sure that if he can get a good idea of what to do, then he can do it himself because ideas are like science. You don't have to be big to use them. And the best kind of idea would be a science idea because science is what makes a song come out of a radio. Or a tuning fork vibrate without touching it. Luis bets it can make a fat *cabron* miss a party, too.

The night before his Confirmation, Luis is in the backseat of the BMW, waiting for Miss Delia to close up the Bubble across the street. While he waits, he practices his prayers for the ceremony. He's timed it, and he can say the Act of Contrition in fifteen seconds flat, no peeking at the book. He's ready.

This afternoon, Abuelita sent Luis home with three huge platters of food that she and her friends cooked after hours, right there in the Hosea House kitchen. When Luis brought the food in, Junior told him that he better not be planning to invite any relatives over after Confirmation, and Luis said no way, which is the truth. It was Abuelita who called everyone.

Luis has to fast now, which means he can't eat anything until his party tomorrow to show that he's willing to suffer for God. As of midnight, he'll be a man, and God will be on his side. He knows his prayers. He's got a suit, and he's got a fistful of sleepy-time for Junior. Thirty-six Vicodin he took out of the big bottle by his mama's bed. The label on the bottle said one every six hours, which is four a day, but Junior's huge, and it takes a lot to stop him from doing what he wants to do. Luis figures he's only gonna have one shot at getting Junior out of the way, so he's gonna give him all thirty-six at once. Enough to make him sleep through the party and maybe a couple of extra days. That way Luis will have time to get the BMW going, and he and his mama can drive off, maybe get to California, but for sure be long gone before Junior wakes up.

Across the street, Luis watches Miss Delia lock the Bubble up. "See you tomorrow!" she says, giving Luis a wave and riding off on her bike. Once she's out of sight, Luis reaches under the front seat and pulls out a bottle of Baileys Irish Cream, borrowed from Abuelita's. It's the most important ingredient for the party tomorrow. Pushing open the car door, he drains most of the bottle into the gutter, leaving just enough to fill Junior's special drink glass.

Luis unties a camouflage bandana with a jawbreaker-sized knot of Vicodin powder in it. Yesterday in science class, while the Giant was getting her nails done, Luis used his compass and a ruler to smash all the pills into tiny bits on the bandana. He twisted that pile of powder into a knot and tied it around his neck. Since then, that knot's been beating with the pulse in his throat: Joon-yer, Joon-yer, Joon-yer. Luis drops the powder a pinch at a time into the bottle. After each pinch, he heats the liquid with a lighter—an old silver one that Junior stole off one of the Idiots—then shakes the bottle, hard, until all the pills are dissolved in the milky drink. He's read in his science book that when a solid completely dissolves in a liquid, it becomes a solution.

When Luis walks through the front door just after midnight, Junior is still awake. *COPS* is on the TV; a guy with a bleeding head, who's wearing nothing but a pair of ladies' drawers, is facedown in the street surrounded by the police. It's over for him.

From the plate on his lap, Junior is tossing *flauta*s into his mouth. Bing, bang, boom, that *cabron* is wrecking the neat pyramid that Abuelita made with the food. He looks over at Luis, his eyes all googly and red. "Whatchu got there, *hijo*?" he asks when he catches sight of the bottle Luis is carrying.

"Nothin."

"Look like some expensive nothin to me. Whatchu doin with that?" Junior digs under the platter of food, pulls his glass from between his legs.

"Abuelita said it's a Confirmation present for my mama," Luis answers, already thinking of his party, his new suit, Abuelita grilling the chicken he hid in the vegetable drawer.

"Look like you already had you some."

"No, sir. She just sent this little bit."

"Fuckin *cholo*s," Junior says, his head bobbing like a balloon on his neck. "Better give me that, then, and don't say nothin to your mama." Junior motions for Luis to open the bottle, shoves his glass out to be filled.

"No, sir," Luis says, emptying the bottle into the glass, "I won't say a thing." He goes over and stands next to the door and watches Junior kill the drink in a few greedy gulps, then Luis drags the milk crate over to a place where he can see the TV.

"Loser!" Junior yells at the guy on *COPS* who's hiding under a plastic swimming pool. The two cops who've been chasing him shake their heads at the half-assed job the junkie's done. His foot is sticking out right where they're standing.

By the time the credits roll on the second of the back-to-back episodes, Junior's face has tipped up toward the ceiling, and he's snorting and snoring. Luis goes over and takes the plate off his lap. He does his best to stack what's left of the *flauta*s the way Abuelita had them, then takes them back to the refrigerator where they belong. He scrubs Junior's drink glass, runs hot water into it, then polishes it with a clean dish towel and puts it away in the cupboard.

Back in the living room, Luis grabs the remote off Junior's stomach. He flips through the channels until he comes to a show about how bridges get built. On the TV, a smart-looking man in khakis and glasses studies his plans, big blue drawings on a table he set up right at the edge of a cliff.

The water is so far down and so wide, it gives Luis the willies to think about it. Rocks poke out of the ground everywhere, and there must be snakes, too. For sure no place to stand when it comes time to start building. Luis can't imagine how anyone could make a way to get over all that mess. But sure enough, an hour into the program, the man with the glasses stands pointing across the completed bridge. Luis watches him get into a car, wave to the crowd, then drive to the other side.

sh athing. He goes over and smells [illegible] and watches [illegible] [illegible], [illegible] a few careful [illegible] then Lane [illegible] [illegible] to a place where he can see the TV.

[illegible] Junior [illegible] the [illegible] plastic swimming pool. The [illegible] [illegible] [illegible] [illegible] [illegible] [illegible] [illegible] [illegible] [illegible] [illegible] [illegible] [illegible] [illegible] [illegible] [illegible] when they're [illegible].

By the time the credits roll on [illegible] the back [illegible] [illegible] Junior's face [illegible] up toward the ceiling, with [illegible] and [illegible]. Lane gets over and [illegible] plate off [illegible]. He doesn't [illegible] to [illegible] what's [illegible] the [illegible] the way. [illegible] [illegible], then takes them back to the [illegible] [illegible] they [illegible] [illegible] [illegible] into a [illegible] glass [illegible] hot [illegible] [illegible] it with a [illegible] towel and [illegible] it away in the cupboard.

Back in the living room, Lane [illegible] the [illegible] on Junior's stomach. He flips through the channels until he comes to a show about [illegible] bridges. [illegible] [illegible] a [illegible] looking man in [illegible] and [illegible] [illegible] [illegible] [illegible] [illegible] [illegible] [illegible] [illegible] [illegible] [illegible] [illegible] of [illegible].

The [illegible] [illegible] and [illegible] [illegible]. [illegible] to think [illegible]. Rocks [illegible] out of the ground [illegible] and there must be [illegible] [illegible] [illegible] [illegible] [illegible] time to start building. [illegible] how anyone could make a way to get over all that [illegible] [illegible] [illegible] into the [illegible] [illegible] with the glass [illegible] across the [illegible] [illegible] [illegible] [illegible] [illegible] [illegible] [illegible] [illegible] to the [illegible] [illegible] [illegible] [illegible].

Acknowledgments

I could not have written these stories without the support of my teachers at the University of New Orleans—Rick Barton, Amanda Boyden, Joseph Boyden, Randy Bates and Joanna Leake—and I will be forever grateful for the countless ways that each of them has helped me.

I am thankful as well to my fellow UNO writers, to those who went before me and shone a light: Bill Loehfelm, A. C. Lambeth and Trip McCormick. To those who went with me: Rachel Trujillo, Jen Violi, Lish McBride, Jason Buch, Amanda Pederson, Pete Syverson and Matt Peters. And to the Big Table Workshop: Arin Black, Chrystopher Masaki Kamakawahine Darkwater, David Parker Jr., Casey Lefante and Carolyn Mikulencak. All lent a bright critical eye and a whole lot of heart to this manuscript.

I am grateful to Dawn Logsdon and to Kay Sanchez, both of whom provided some essential education and inspiration.

Marcus, Matt, Tom and Kendall Johnson were my road in, my way out. And my Bean family: all roads lead to you. There is nowhere I will ever be that is half as good as any place you are.

I thank the editors at *Glimmer Train Stories*, *Washington Square* and *Greensboro Review* for giving my early writing a place to live. Grants from the Astraea Foundation enabled me to spend more time writing. And the Gift of Freedom award from A Room of Her Own Foundation has supported parts of this book and will make it possible to write the next one. I am grateful beyond measure.

The fact of this book belongs to my agent, the dynamic Michael Murphy, and to the genius of my editor, Michael Signorelli, and the vision of my publisher, Carrie Kania.

About the author

About the book

Read on

Insights,
Interviews
& More . . .

About the author

Meet Barb Johnson

I GREW UP in Lake Charles, Louisiana, in a semirural setting. Back then, what land wasn't devoted to rice and soybeans was occupied by oil and natural gas wells. A couple of those wells clanked away on the other side of the back fence at my elementary school. Lots of kids dream of their schools burning to the ground, and we were no different, except for us, fire was an ever-present possibility. Those wells could be counted on to blow up from time to time, and when they did, it took a little doing to put the fire out.

It was a combustible place, my hometown, and I was always antsy to leave it. I remember staring at the cloudy black chalkboard of my second-grade classroom and thinking, *only ten more years.* What in the world would make an eight-year-old think such a thing? Books, most likely. They lit my imagination with stories of big cities and apartments in old buildings, where bright lights might drown out the heavy beam of the moon that rode just above the fields near my house.

P. B. Baldwin

About the minute I graduated high school, I packed a paper sack full of clothes and grabbed my guitar. I didn't have any particular plan except to see what else there was in the world, the real world. I somehow landed in Larchmont, New York, working as a governess. *Governess* sounds glamorous. Who doesn't think of *The Sound of Music* when they hear the word? But in fact, what I was doing in Larchmont was no different than what I would've been doing had I stayed in Lake Charles: I was taking care of other people's kids and cleaning their house. I didn't have much talent for either.

I was eighteen and couldn't imagine being let into college, had no idea how college worked, but I assumed it had nothing to do with people like me. I got most of my education by taking the train into the city. Walking through Manhattan, I tried to affect sophistication, but I hadn't quite mastered the lack of eye contact that is the hallmark of city dwellers. This made me a magnet for the unhinged, who hunger to be looked at directly now and then, and I was happy to receive their strange lessons. Once, a small man sweeping the sidewalk in Central Park—in no official capacity that I could tell—gave me an hour-long seminar on Padre Pio. Another time, a heroin addict with full casts on both arms showed me how she was still able to shoot up.

I moved around for a while after that time, until, eventually, I ended up in New Orleans, where I found an apartment in a beautiful old building. I even managed to get myself into college. The whole time I was there, I kept waiting for someone to tap me on the shoulder and say, "Miss Johnson, I'm afraid there's been a mistake." And then I'd be escorted off campus and given bus fare to the TG&Y, where I would apply for a job in Ladies' Notions. This occupation would combine three of the things I feared most in life: the very idea of *ladies' notions,* working inside under fluorescent lighting, and sales. So great was my fear of such a job, it outlived the five-and-dime store that inspired it.

While I was in college, a couple of my teachers said some really nice things about my writing, said maybe I should pursue it. I liked writing, but it wasn't a job, as far as I could tell. If I was going to stay in school, I needed money. I'd heard that painters made twice the minimum wage, so I got myself hired as a house painter. Every day I climbed two stories up a ladder to work in the full, hot sun of a July in New Orleans. That was deep Hades, let me tell you. The wind ▸

Meet Barb Johnson ***(continued)***

was even worse than the heat. I only weighed a buck fifteen, and the slightest breeze could lift the ladder free of the house. My job consisted entirely of scraping off loose lead paint by hand. *Screep-screep-screeeep,* I inched my way along that gigantic house with a rusty paint scraper. I have a flair for monotony, I do, but that was the limit for me. One day I went inside the house and made myself useful to the carpenter, and, eventually, I got a carpentry gig in exactly the same way I had gotten the painting job, by exaggerating my level of expertise. "Are you an experienced carpenter?" the contractor asked. "Yessir," I said. "Look at my circular saw." And so I became a carpenter.

Twenty years passed before I put that saw down and picked up a laptop and began to write seriously. At first, I tried to write about the world I had read about, what I considered to be the real world—stories about well-educated people crippled by ennui. Then I enrolled in an MFA program, where I finally returned to the subjects I know best: gay girls and oil refineries, fatherless boys stuck in the maze, alienated people living off the grid, and folks who sit in abandoned cars to do their serious thinking.

When I read, I have realized, I read to escape where I am. When I write, though, I write to return to where I've been. And when I return, the heavy moon that once rode low over my past—that same old moon—turns magically into the high, bright illumination upon which every writer the world over depends.

Barb Johnson has been a carpenter in New Orleans for more than twenty years. In 2008, she received her MFA from the University of New Orleans. While there, she won a grant from the Astraea Foundation, Glimmer Train*'s Short Story Award for New Writers, and* Washington Square*'s short story competition. In 2009, she became the fifth recipient of A Room of Her Own Foundation's $50,000 Gift of Freedom. She lives and writes in New Orleans. This is her first book.*

About the Book

It seems inconceivable to me now, but the majority of the stories in this book were written right on the heels of Hurricane Katrina. They were not written to describe the disaster—there's not a peep about that old storm in these pages. They were created as a means to transcend the horror of the immediate by casting an eye back in time on the place I love best. Denial is one of my greatest skills, and writing makes very good use of it. The stories were often written in unusual places and certainly under fairly bizarre circumstances. In the end, I guess, their existence proves that we are designed to carry on. Our ability to imagine, to believe in a world we cannot see, is our greatest asset, the source of our most profound strength.

For nearly twenty years before Katrina wiped it out, I had my carpentry workshop in an old rented warehouse in Mid-City New Orleans. The year before the hurricane, I'd decided that I'd enroll in an MFA program if they'd have me, and, luckily, they would and they did. For that whole year before the storm, I went back and forth about getting out of the carpentry business. In an instant the issue became moot because every single tool and piece of salvaged historic architecture in my shop was completely ruined in the flood.

The University of New Orleans, where ▸

I was in the MFA program—the Creative Writing Workshop—was heavily damaged, and we were all spread out around the country. Then something very amazing began to happen. One person found another, and that one led to another, and pretty soon—in a little over a month after the storm—UNO had risen up and recreated itself online, the only university in the city to resume classes that semester.

Two weeks after the storm, I sneaked back into the city with a friend and saw that I could live on my apartment's balcony. A couple of weeks later, I did just that. During the day, I'd drive around looking for a place to charge my laptop and to download my classmates' stories. At night, I'd read those stories and work on my own. There was no one anywhere. The whole neighborhood was dark and empty. Except for the stink and the heat and the mosquitoes, it was beautiful at night. Like being out in the country. The darkness provided a relief from the visual assault that went with life in the daylight: debris everywhere, pieces of my neighbors' lives sitting in the middle of the street, animals that hadn't made it through the storm.

Black Hawk helicopters and big fat jets, flying below radar, circled the city day and night. Every evening, the National Guard drove by in what they called their "heavily armed golf carts," actual golf carts put into service for patrols. These were young guys still in their teens carrying M16s. Every day, they'd say the same thing when they saw me. "Ma'am," they'd say, "you can't be here. This neighborhood hasn't been okayed for occupancy." And I'd say, "Yes, I know." Then they'd wave and drive off, and I'd go back to writing.

"Killer Heart," one of the stories in this collection, is set in the Irish Channel, a New Orleans neighborhood that didn't flood. I worked on it mostly at night under a mosquito net while wearing a headlamp. At the time, I couldn't imagine my own neighborhood, Mid-City, any other way than the way it was: empty, stinking, everything dead. So, as sad as "Killer Heart" is, I will always remember it as providing me with a happy picture of the city I love as it was before the storm—an imaginative slant that was absolutely necessary to my sanity.

Anyone who was in the city at that time was starving for something normal—seeing a neighbor, walking the dog, sitting down to a meal with friends. Writing was the only thing I did after the storm that I'd done before it. It was normal. Having to write under those circumstances banished forever any notion that things had to be a certain way—neat desk, good coffee, agreeable temperature—in order for me to write. When I began to write about squabbling couples and a boy who worried about the Holy Spirit, I was pretty sure that I was going to be fine. What's more normal than bickering and the damaging effects of catechism on a young mind?

In January of 2006, four months after the hurricane, UNO's classes once again met on campus. The whole city was still torn up and functioning only marginally. As it always had, our writing workshop met at night, and a trip to school meant a pitch-black drive across the city and out to the lake. No stop lights. Roadways often narrowed by fallen trees and snagged detritus. Only a rough path was cleared for cars. Upended boats were left trying to climb the trees and buildings they'd floated up to. A wrecked helicopter hugged the bayou, a FOR RENT sign posted in its window.

Along the canal next to school, a chunk of damaged levee was being repaired. At night, the city filled with an intense blackness, which, on campus, was barely mitigated by two generator-powered klieg lights, fireflies lighting a vast ocean of darkness. The building in which we met was powered by a generator, too, and its rooms were pretty wrecked. No ceiling tiles. No floor tiles. No overhead lights. No heat. No air-conditioning. No toilets.

During the day, workers bagged mildewed paper and books and used our classroom as a central drop-off for debris. We often began that class by dragging trash bags out to the Dumpster. In that room, the windows ran floor to ceiling, and the glass doors opened onto a courtyard. I remember one evening it was raining lightly. People were still skittish from the storm and frequently burst into tears when it rained or when they saw water of any kind. Still, in the fading light, our teacher opened the doors so we could hear the raindrops hitting the broad leaves of the elephant ear plants outside. He read to us something he'd been looking at before class, something that had struck him as beautiful. I can't remember what it was, but the ▸

combined effect of being read to and the rain—just for that moment—sounding pleasant again, well, people cried from the relief of it.

Finishing the writing program, for which this group of stories was my thesis, took a year longer than I'd planned, but I was thankful for that extra time. Writing this now, I think of my oldest brother, who made origami and fashioned trivets from gum wrappers to get over what he'd seen during the war. These stories provided that same kind of therapy for me because they simultaneously distracted me and forced me to think about the larger concerns in life. They kept my hands busy and corralled my mind when it bucked and kicked and threatened to run off.

Notes in the Wall

WHEN I WAS A CARPENTER, every time I renovated a house, I would save the pieces I was removing—antique baseboard, old sash windows—and then put them in another house, a sort of architectural cross-pollination. Then I'd leave a note inside the wall or the window casing for future carpenters. They were simple notes, mostly, explaining what I had done to the structure, where the antique window or baseboard had come from. That's what unfamiliar details in a book do, I think. They serve as little bits of cultural cross-pollination. In reading Margaret Atwood, for example, I learned about Eaton's department store. In *The Grapes of Wrath*, it was the Hoovervilles. There were knots in Annie Proulx's *Shipping News.* The ha-ha in Ian McEwan's *Atonement.* When I come across those sorts of details, I am always delighted to learn more about them. With this in mind, I've pulled some of the details from this collection of stories—mostly those that people have asked about.

CLACKERS: INNOCENT FUN OR PURE EVIL?

People who read the story "More of This World or Maybe Another" often ask about Clackers. Ninety-nine percent martial arts weapon, this child's toy from the early seventies comprised two balls, approximately two inches in diameter and made of very dense and fairly brittle ▸

Read on

acrylic plastic. Imagine attaching one of these balls to either end of a twenty-four-inch shoestring. In the center, thread the shoestring through a flat washer to form a generous, one-inch gripping surface, and we're talking hours of fun for little Suzy. The point of Clackers (if they can be said to have a point) was to rock that washer up and down until the Clackers smacked together and made the sort of ear-piercing noise that is the raison d'être of children everywhere. Were flying shards of acrylic a hazard? Was swinging those dense orbs in a crowd dangerous? Some saw it that way. But there wasn't a kid worth his salt who wasn't curious to see how fast he could make those Clackers fly, how hard he could smack them together before they'd just break apart completely. Shattered Clackers, then, were merely a sign of a child's healthy curiosity. And if a kid got a black eye from standing too close to someone with Clackers, everyone agreed it said more about the kid than about the toy. This is what made the seventies so great: the nearly complete absence of personal-injury lawsuits.

YOU SAY POMMES DE TERRE, I SAY PATATE

In "If the Holy Spirit Comes for You," a young Dooley counts in his head *un patate, deux patate* when he gets nervous. *Patate* is the Cajun French (and French vernacular) word for potato. The French French word is the unwieldy *pommes de terre,* apples of the earth. Not so long ago, Cajun children often used *patate* in the one-potato, two-potato rhyme most kids in the U.S. use to decide who's it or who's out. Imagine using *pomme de terre* for that: *un pomme de terre, deux pommes de terre, trois pommes de terre . . .* Most kids would ditch that game *tout de suite.* But *un patate, deux patate* has a nice rhythm. Just as there is Spanglish in the U.S.—*bistec,* say—there is Franglish in southwest Louisiana, hence *patate.*

A SHOTGUN HOUSE IS NOT LIKE A SHOTGUN WEDDING

In "Killer Heart," Dooley lives in a shotgun house in the Irish Channel section of New Orleans. Because New Orleans was built along a crescent-shaped turn in the Mississippi—it's not called the Crescent

City for nothing—the lots tend to be long and narrow. The perfect house for such a lot is the shotgun house, so called because, if you were of a mind to, you could fire a shotgun through the front door and the shot would exit through the back door unimpeded. I applied this same logic the first time I came across the phrase *railroad flat*. Clearly, a railroad flat was a long, narrow house through which a train could enter the front and roll straight out the back without interruption, an event only slightly less likely than someone firing a shotgun through the front door and running around back to admire his handiwork. The shotgun house is, in fact, a humble building in which each room leads directly to the next. No side rooms. No hallway.

Inexpensive to build, these houses were often constructed of barge board reclaimed from vessels that made one-way trips down the Mississippi. For the modern dweller, life in a shotgun house means somebody's going to be walking through your bedroom on the way to the bathroom or to get a snack. Along with kitchens, bathrooms were often tacked on to the back of the house, because shotguns were mostly built between the 1860s and the 1920s, before indoor plumbing became the norm for those of modest means.

WHEN THE GOING GETS TOUGH, THE TOUGH GET A PIMM'S CUP

When life in a narrow shotgun house gets too, well, *narrow*, there's nothing like a long, tall Pimm's Cup, a beverage that is consumed in the story "Issue Is." To enjoy the full effect of this drink, you must take yourself to England, or, failing that, to the Napoleon House in New Orleans. With the right ingredients, you can enjoy the almost-full effect in the comfort of your own home.

Pimm's is a gin-based alcoholic beverage with a spicy, kind of fruity thing going on. Only it's subtle, because it's British. There's almost nothing British in New Orleans, most especially not at the Napoleon House, but on a hot day, when your knickers are sticking to you, there's nothing more refreshing.

At the Napoleon House, they use a tall, slender glass that feels ▸

Notes in the Wall ***(continued)***

like the 1920s in your hand because big, modern American portions don't lend themselves to slender glasses. In any case, find the glass. It's important. Fill this twelve-ounce glass with ice and add 1¼ ounces Pimm's No. 1 and three ounces of lemonade. Fill the rest with—and try not to let this blow the magic for you—7Up or Fresca or Sprite or, if you're feeling really old school, ginger ale. The ginger ale will make you feel fancy. Try it. The most important, most refreshing element of the Pimm's Cup (not more refreshing than how you'll soon be forgetting your cares, of course) is the cucumber slice with which the drink should be garnished. The cucumber is a fruit, and fruit is good for you; ergo, the Pimm's Cup is a healthy lifestyle choice.